THE
TUDDLEBY
TRAIT

JANINE FAITH GOODMAN

Illustrated by Aliza Horowitz

To Gil, Orly and Oren
for all your love and support.
You are the magic makers
in my world.

THE
TUDDLEBY
TRAIT

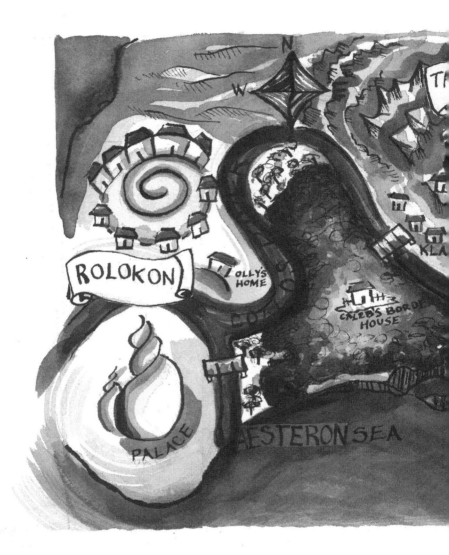

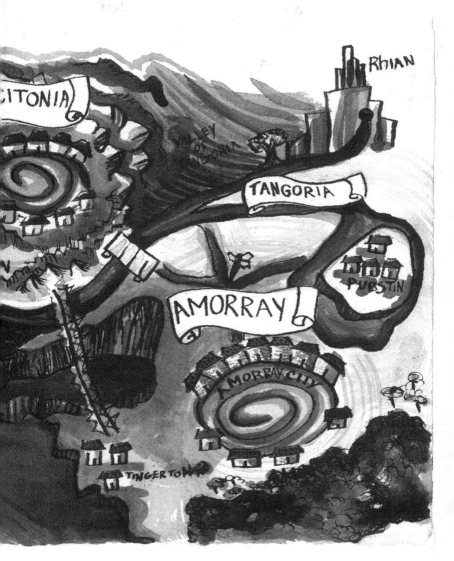

The Adventure Begins

The evening was turning out a whole lot differently than eleven-year-old Tommy Tuddleby could have ever imagined.

It began when he'd picked a spot in his backyard and started to dig. His uncle had told him there was a secret tunnel and possibly even pirate treasure buried behind the house. Tommy was going to find them. He had done some exploring when they'd first moved in a couple of months ago. He'd only dug a few inches when his mom made him stop. But Tommy had read in *Jake Jones, Private*

Investigator, his go-to book, that you have to be persistent, and if there's one thing Tommy could be, it was persistent.

Finding a treasure would really impress the kids at his new school—which was a top priority for Tommy, since the first day of sixth grade was approaching fast. First impressions are key to success, Jake Jones always said. And Jake Jones always knew what he was talking about.

Unfortunately, his mother had a different perspective.

"Tommy!" she called out from the kitchen just as he pushed his shovel into the grass. "What in the world are you doing to my lawn! I've told you before. No digging!"

Tommy looked up, startled. "Uh . . . Uncle Thomas said there was gold buried here, and I figured—"

"Well," she interrupted, "Uncle Thomas isn't the one who's going to have to repair the lawn. So find something less . . . destructive to do." Her face disappeared from the window and then reappeared a second later. "And take off that jacket before you overheat!"

"But Mom!" The old brown jacket and scuffed cowboy boots were his adventuring gear. Over his shoulder he had slung an olive-green canvas satchel containing the five "must-haves" Jake Jones said you should travel with at *all* times: high-resolution compact binoculars, a seven-in-one survival whistle, a five-in-one pocket knife, an invisible pen with UV blacklight key chain and pad of paper, and a snack. The snack was Pop Rocks, which his mom said didn't count—but Jake Jones says, "Adventuring may be serious business, but you don't have to be serious *all* the time." He didn't have a flashlight, but he did have his Harry Potter illuminating wand ready for when he reached the tunnel. And being short and skinny might actually work to his advantage for once.

"*Now*, Tommy," Mom said.

Tommy wrinkled his nose and scowled. He replaced the shovel where he had found it, put his wand in his back pocket, and went inside.

Mom sighed at his glum expression. "It's that Tuddleby trait!" she said. "You just can't be happy sitting quietly, can you? Even for a moment! Come to think of it, for days I've been telling you to clean your room. Now seems the perfect time." She looked him over. "Who knows, you might even find a few treasures underneath all that mess," she added with a wink.

"Well, if I have to be in my room cleaning, then I might as well go to bed when I'm done," Tommy replied petulantly.

She looked at him, surprised, as she placed the last of the dinner dishes in the dishwasher. "So soon?"

"It's not that early." He turned and headed out of the room, mumbling, "Anyway, my dreams are probably a lot more fun."

"Especially in a clean room," Mom called out after him.

UNCLE THOMAS WOULD HAVE LET ME INVESTIGATE, TOMMY thought as he trudged up the stairs. He was the most adventuresome person Tommy could think of—besides Jake Jones, of course.

Uncle Thomas had traveled all over the world for a while, but he eventually moved back in with Tommy's grandparents and settled down to help Tommy's grandfather with the family hardware store. He still took weekend trips to really cool places, though, which is how he met Aunt Rej, who everyone else in his family jokingly called "Aunt Red" because of her shocking bright-red hair. When Grandpa and Grandma moved to a retirement home, Uncle Thomas talked Tommy's parents into taking over the store, and then last June he and Aunt Red packed up most of their belongings, handed over the house keys to Tommy's father, and moved to Colorado, where the air was clean and the snow was plentiful. Aunt Red had never seen snow before.

Going to his room wasn't actually *so* bad. It was a lot bigger than where he'd slept in his old apartment, *and* he didn't have to share it with his little sister, Tina, who was a huge pain in the neck. Plus he'd found a book of short stories that Uncle Thomas had left behind in the back of the closet. Tommy had read one—an old-fashioned adventure that was sort of interesting—and the next story *did* look kind of exciting. He'd get to cleaning . . . eventually.

But it all went wrong when Tommy reached the top of the stairs and found that the door to his bedroom was shut tight. "Really?" he grumbled. "Not again!" He had forgotten to leave his door open a crack, and the summer heat had swelled the wooden door frame.

He turned the doorknob and pushed. The door wouldn't budge. He jiggled the knob, banged his fists against the door, and kicked it, which was rather painful. The door remained stuck.

As he paused to consider a new strategy, he heard funny snorting noises and odd sighs from the other side. Someone was messing with him. Tina! The game was on!

"Let me in!" Tommy demanded, shoving the door with his shoulder.

"Ahem, yes? Stop making such a racket," scolded a gruff voice from the other side of the door. "For future reference, I respond only to polite gestures."

That sure didn't *sound* like Tina. She might say something like that, but even she couldn't change her voice that much. *I bet it's Dad playing a joke,* he thought. *It wouldn't be the first time!*

"May I come in?" Tommy asked, as sweetly as he could.

"What's the password?" the voice demanded.

"How am I supposed to know?" Tommy laughed. "After all, it's *my* bedroom. I've never needed a password."

"The password!"

"But I really don't know," said Tommy, growing frustrated. "Come on, Dad, let me in!"

"I am not your father. Now come, the password."

"But . . ."

"Tommy," his mother called from the kitchen, "who are you talking to, dear?"

"No one, Mom," he replied.

"What a thing to say!" the voice behind the door growled. "No one? Humph! Why, how do you ever expect to open this door with such an attitude?"

"Well, it's just that . . ." Flustered, Tommy stopped midsentence. Was it really his father on the other side of the door? He sounded . . . different.

"Yes?" the voice said expectantly.

Tommy grumbled under his breath, "You'd have this attitude too if you were always being told you can't do what you want to do!" Then he added, louder, "You've left me no choice, Dad! I've got my wand. And I know just the magic spell to use!" Tommy whipped out the wand from his back pocket and sternly called out the words Uncle Thomas had taught him when they played Battle of the Wands: "Mochachocolatexpresso!"

("It's foolproof," Uncle Thomas had told him. "Works every time." Most of the time it didn't, actually. In fact, almost never. But it was the first thing that came to mind.)

Tommy turned the knob and pushed hard on the door at the same time. And his bedroom door opened, sending him tumbling through.

"Ah, there we go! That works just as well. Hmm, you're not what I expected. Rather young, aren't you? A bit small. But then again, no one ever described what you *did* look like."

Tommy caught himself on his nightstand and looked up, startled, confused, and annoyed at being called small for what seemed like the hundredth time.

"You're not so much to look at either!" he retorted, his irritation momentarily winning out.

Indeed, the gruff voice matched the body like the roar of a lion coming from a mouse. Five feet away and a few inches shorter than Tommy stood a round little man with pale gray skin. He was dressed all in black and white, with a tall top hat, a tailcoat, and baggy pants that looked as if they were going to slip right off. The little man felt through his pockets. "Fiddlesticks! I can't find my pocket watch, and I'm worried we're running late. Have you the time?"

Tommy gazed nervously around his room, figuring out his next move. On the one hand, yelling for his parents seemed like a wise choice. But the little man seemed harmless enough—though his gray skin was a bit weird—and once his parents got involved, things would get a lot less interesting. The key question, as always, was: What would

Jake Jones do? And Tommy immediately knew the answer. He'd handle this. At least for now.

"Hey, mister, who are you? What are you doing in my room? And what do you mean *'we're running late'*? Late for what?" Tommy demanded, holding out his wand menacingly and straightening up so he was as tall as possible.

"Never mind all that. We'll talk later. Now, have you the time?" repeated the little man, pointing to the band circling Tommy's wrist. Tommy looked down. Uncle Thomas had given it to him when he moved in and it did look kind of like a watch. The band connected to a round clasp adorned with cool symbols all in a circle. But there were no hands or numbers.

"I'm sorry. It's not a watch," replied Tommy, irritated at being ignored.

"Really?" said the little man skeptically. "Well, then, double fiddlesticks. Perhaps you have a belt? I forgot to put one on this morning." He hiked up his pants with the hand that held a wooden cane and clutched a second black top hat with the other hand.

Tommy popped his wand into his satchel and searched through his drawers and his closet, but he found no belt large enough to fit around the little man's pudgy waist.

"Oh well," sighed the little man. "We'll just hope the wind isn't too harsh, or that we won't have to run from a rain shower, for then my pants might fall down, which would be very unpleasant indeed!"

"Wind?" Tommy exclaimed with surprise. "There's no wind."

"We'll fix that in no time." The little man held up the second hat. "Put this on, and we'll be off."

"It looks a little too big for me. And besides, what do I need it for?" Tommy asked.

"Stop asking so many questions," the little man said, exasperated. "Ah, there you are," he said, patting his vest pocket. His hand disappeared inside his tailcoat and reappeared holding a small pocket watch. He clicked open the case and shook his head. "We *are* running late. Well, come on!" He held the hat out to Tommy. Tommy opened his mouth to ask another question, but the little man rolled his eyes, flipped the hat over, and replaced Tommy's baseball cap with the top hat.

The hat fell right over Tommy's eyes. The ground seemed to slip away from beneath his feet, and air rushed past him at lightning speed. Tommy immediately felt queasy in the pit of his stomach and dizzy in his head. He was sure he'd topple over, but he didn't. Then the ground settled comfortably beneath his feet once again, and the queasy feeling subsided.

"Oof!" Tommy exclaimed. "That did *not* feel good. What just happened?" He pulled the hat off his head. His eyes widened in confusion, and his mouth dropped open.

"Where in the world am I? And what happened to my room?"

Indeed, these were good questions to ask, for Tommy now stood in a room very different from his own. He saw a table with some papers on it and a wooden chair tucked underneath and a bowl of what looked like oranges . . . except they weren't orange. They were a mousy gray. The only light came from a torch hanging out from the wall. Tommy ran over to a window. It was dim outside, and all he could see was the silhouette of mountains in the distance and a nearby road that disappeared around a small hill. There were no cars, no trucks, no bicycles, no big glass buildings. Nothing looked familiar. He turned around and scanned the room again. He then looked down at his brown boots and blue jeans and the green satchel still slung across his shoulder. Finally he looked at the little gray man, who was now sitting in the chair. Tommy swallowed.

"And what . . . what happened to all the color?"

The Color Guard Tells His Tale

Your room still exists," the little man stated matter-of-factly. "And you are quite correct—this is a world without color. Welcome to the land of Rolokon in the kingdom of Aesteron." He looked puzzled at the astonished look on Tommy's face. "I would have thought you'd know." He shrugged. "Well, never mind. We'd best be off." He rose from the chair, lifted the torch from its holder, and walked toward the door.

Tommy did not move. "I'm not going anywhere until you answer my questions!"

The little man stopped and turned around. "Hmm?"

"Who are you?"

"My full name is Sir Horatio Piebald Hue, Esquire."

"Why 'Esquire'?"

"Because I like it. Now that's two questions. Are you quite finished?"

"No!" Tommy said angrily. "Where are we going? And what is this business about having no color?"

Horatio's eyes widened. "Calm yourself, Mr. Tuddleby! No need to be so rude!"

Tommy swallowed, fighting back nausea. He wasn't sure if he was still sick from traveling inside a hat or if the gravity of his odd situation was hitting home. His mind raced. He had always wanted a real adventure, but this was crazy. Unless he was dreaming. *Dreams can be pretty crazy,* he thought. *If this is a dream, then I'm really still at home. I must have fallen asleep, and this is all in my head.*

He took a deep breath and looked up at Horatio. This was just a dream. He could do this.

"I'm so sorry. I didn't mean to be rude," Tommy said as calmly as he could. "Please go on."

Horatio nodded and led Tommy out the door.

They set off down the road, and as they rounded a curve, Tommy saw a steep hill ahead.

"You'll see where we're going once we reach the hilltop. But about the color—" Horatio paused. "Perhaps it *is* best I begin to explain." He took Tommy's arm and urged him on, but their pace slowed as he spoke.

"A week ago, our land was filled with colors beautiful and bright. The sunsets were perhaps the most divine of all, with oranges and purples and fiery reds and yellows. Even the clouds overhead were each tinted a bit differently. And now nothing.

"Don't think all these colors just appeared," he added quickly, "because they didn't. We have, or at least *had*, a color guard named Olly. Soon I'll take you to see him."

Horatio paused to wipe away the perspiration that beaded on his forehead and trickled down his cheeks. "It's so dreadfully hot out. This is the warm season in Rolokon, but it's never been like this!"

"I have to say," Tommy said, panting as they climbed higher, "it's hot at home, but nowhere near this hot!"

"And it is always so dark now!" Horatio added. "During the day, thick black clouds block the sun. At least at night we have the light of the moons." Tommy looked up and saw three small round circles of light beaming down at them. "I can't help but think all these changes must have *something* to do with losing our color."

Once they reached the hilltop, the entire colorless land spread out before them. Horatio pointed out the marketplace at the center of clusters of houses and then the Collos, the main river, which wound in and around the land and spilled into a large body of water that Horatio called the

Aesteron Sea. Nestled between the Collos and the Aesteron Sea was a grand palace, partly concealed by tall trees. Tommy looked along the river's course to the right of the palace and saw a foreboding forest.

"Gosh, the forest looks pretty creepy. Are we going to have to go in there?" he asked.

"I suspect so," replied Horatio.

"What's on the other side of it?"

"The other lands of the kingdom. There are four in all."

"So you have to cross the river to reach them?"

"Yes." Horatio nodded. "Over one of the bridges."

Tommy gazed out at the water and then across the rest of the land. "My," he said softly, "what a very sad place to live in."

"Yes, it is a sad place." Horatio shook his head and sighed. "We have a difficult job ahead of us."

"Job?" Tommy asked.

"Yes indeed."

"What am *I* supposed to do?"

"I'm surprised you haven't used your . . . uh . . . abilities to understand all this already. Why do you think I came for you? You're going to help us *find* color."

"I didn't even know anyone could lose color. And I've never had to look for anything so—so big. I'm pretty good at finding things that get lost around our house. But color? It's really not the same."

"No, but I'm sure you can do it. What about one of those spells or charms or whatever you wizards do?"

"What?" Tommy asked, puzzled.

"You *are* Thomas Tuddleby, the wayfaring wizard of whimsy, magic maker and spellbreaker, are you not?" Horatio slapped his hand over his forehead and groaned. "Don't tell me!?"

"Yes, my name *is* Tommy Tuddleby. I just never thought of myself as a wizard," he said, rather pleased with the title.

"Well, if you have the right name and you were in the right place, then you must be the right person, and that's all that counts. If you prefer, I won't refer to you as a wizard."

"No, I don't mind being a wizard at all."

"You do think your magic can help, don't you?" Horatio asked hopefully.

"Yes, of ... of course ..." Tommy thought quickly. "It's just I—I'm not your everyday wizard, and it may take me some time ... but I can solve this!" He nearly convinced himself. *It's a dream, after all.* Though a remarkably vivid one.

"Indeed!" exclaimed Horatio, patting Tommy on the back. "By the way, I was quite impressed by that Mocha spell you used. I was beginning to wonder if I'd come to the right place! The password would have also worked, but magic is just as good. In fact, it's what we need! Plus that door was quite stuck. I'm not sure I could have opened it even if you had said the password!"

With that, he hurried Tommy along.

THE PATH THEY WERE ON JOINED A GRAVEL ROAD THAT sloped downhill. Soon they arrived at one of the clusters of houses, and out from one came an unhappy-looking man almost old enough to be Tommy's grandfather.

His head hung low, and there were deep circles under his troubled eyes. His hair was uncombed, and he wore an oversized jacket, long shorts, and sandals. He spotted Tommy and Horatio and trudged dejectedly toward them.

As the tall man neared, Tommy did a double take. The man's jacket was decorated with lots of little eyes that opened and closed—one of them even seemed to look right at him and wink! It took all of Tommy's resolve to focus on the man's face instead.

"Oh, Sir Horatio," the man sobbed, "what in the world am I to do? I can't sleep. I can't eat. And it's so terribly hot out, it's nearly unbearable! Do you think I caused this too?"

"Here's the person we're looking for!" cried Horatio. "There now, Olly," he said soothingly, "I have someone who will be of help. I'd like to introduce you to Thomas Tuddleby."

"*Tommy* Tuddleby," Tommy corrected.

Olly raised his head and looked despairingly at Tommy. "It's very nice to meet you, Mr. Tuddleby, but how are *you* going to help *me*? You're only a little boy, and this is a big problem."

"I'm not a little boy!" Tommy said indignantly. He stood up straight, pushed out his chest, and furrowed his brow, attempting to look as intimidating as possible. In truth, though, Tommy had been thinking similar thoughts. He had no idea how to solve this whole color business.

"Oh!" said Olly. "I didn't mean any offense!" His lips trembled, and tears welled up in his eyes.

Tommy softened. Whether or not he could find the missing color suddenly seemed less important than calming Olly.

"A person can do many things whether he is little or big. I *will* find color for you," he assured Olly. "After all, I'm a w-wayfaring wizard of whimsy . . ." He looked over at Horatio. ". . . magic maker and spellbreaker!" he finished triumphantly.

"Olly," Horatio added quickly, "I want you to explain to Mr. Tuddleby what led to your unfortunate misplacement of color."

"Well, I am the color guard. At least I was," Olly began woefully. "No one in the land has, at least *had*, so important a job. But then, one night—oh dear, oh dear!" Olly broke down and wept. "Oh, Mr. Tuddleby, you must think me a horrible man. I truly didn't intend to lose our color. I love it so. How unforgivable of me!"

Tommy glanced helplessly at Horatio.

"There's nothing to be forgiven, Olly," consoled Horatio. "Just tell Mr. Tuddleby what happened."

Olly raised his head, took a handkerchief from his jacket pocket, and wiped the tears from his eyes.

"One night," he began again, hiccupping every now and then, "my dear friends Mr. and Mrs. Brown were having a lovely party. Do you remember, Sir Horatio? Everyone was invited. I had such a lovely time and stayed quite late. In fact, it was nearing dawn when I remembered my color duties—"

"Why do you have to *guard* color?" Tommy interrupted. "It's always there, isn't it? I mean, it shouldn't make any difference what you do, right?"

"But it does!" Horatio and Olly both exclaimed.

"Long ago," Horatio explained, "when the world was being created, an enchanter provided each land with light and warmth and wind and water so each group of people could care for itself. All was well until, one day, a dark sorcerer found his way to our kingdom and unleashed a terrible curse upon the land. In Rolokon, our color just . . . just vanished, as it has now. Not long after that, a young messenger from a great enchanter appeared and assured us that all would be well. He took from his cloak pocket a small box. Then he walked over to the large river that runs through the center of the land, filled a vial with the river water, clicked open the box, and added a few droplets. Color burst out of the box and filled the land with color—shocking oranges and purples and reds—even more beautiful than before. He closed the box as everyone admired this wondrous event, but when he reopened it, the color swirled back inside, where lay a most magnificent cream-white pearl.

"The messenger said, 'This is the last of the Pearls of Colloster. I have distributed a pearl to each of the other three lands in your kingdom to free them from the sorcerer's curse.' He gave them the box of color and the pearl on several conditions. First, the pearl could only produce the color when three drops of water taken from the Collos River were added to the box each morning. Second, one person would be chosen to guard the pearl and add the water and that responsibility would be passed down through the generations of that family. Third, the messenger cautioned them, 'Do not attempt to seek out the great enchanter. He prefers to remain unknown. Be happy with what he has given to you and your neighboring lands and obey the laws I have decreed, always and forever.'

"The people were eager to bring color back to their land and so readily agreed to his terms. The people chose one sage to be Rolokon's color guard, and they nicknamed him Olly because he loved the color olive green. The messenger for the great enchanter was never seen again," concluded the little man.

"The job has been passed down my family tree to every eldest son," added Olly. "I was named in memory of my great, great, great . . . I don't know *how* great, but certainly very great grandfather. And we have always had color—until now, that is."

"Wow, what a story!" said Tommy. "It reminds me of this story I just read. It's about this place called Ree something and there's an enchanter and an evil guy and—"

"A-*hem*," Horatio interrupted, raising his eyebrows and motioning toward Olly, who was becoming visibly more upset.

Tommy nodded and said, "Being color guard seems like a really big responsibility!"

"It *is*. And the hours are horrible. I wanted to be an adventurer, but as color guard I can never leave the land . . . and I'm just not very good at it."

"Why do you say that?" asked Tommy. "Everyone messes up sometimes."

"Er . . . well, this wasn't exactly the first time. Once I was doing an experiment using the water from a nearby spring and I had a little dropper with water from that spring and then a little dropper with the water from the river . . . and, well . . ." Olly looked down at his shoes.

"Yes?" prompted Tommy.

Olly took a deep breath. "Well, I used water from the wrong dropper on the pearl. That day the colors were all wrong—the trees were green and the sky was blue. They had to stay that way until the next morning when I added the correct river water."

Tommy looked confused. "But isn't that what they're supposed—"

"So *that's* what happened!" interrupted Horatio, shaking his head. "You told me the unusual amount of rain from the night before had affected the river water!"

"Well, I'm sure it did. That's why I was experimenting." Olly looked sheepishly from Tommy to Horatio. "It's just that that wasn't the reason the colors came out all wrong."

Horatio sighed, shaking his head, and turned to Tommy. "I love Olly. We all do. But I can't even count the number of times Olly has misplaced the pearl. So it didn't worry anyone at first when he couldn't find it. But now we are all very concerned, for if the pearl is really and truly lost, then we can never have color again."

"So what happened when you lost it *this* time?" pressed Tommy.

Olly breathed in deeply and continued. "Just as I was about to place the water droplets in the special box, I thought I heard someone calling to me. I followed the voice but couldn't find anyone. And being so very tired and having run in so many directions in search of this mysterious person, I quite lost myself. I must have tripped over something and fallen, for the next thing I remember is waking up to a dark, colorless world. I found my way back, but the pearl was nowhere to be seen, not in my special place, not anywhere!"

"Nowhere?"

"Nowhere. We combed through the whole area. But the pearl is so small that unless it's in my special place, I don't think I *could* find it."

"So *I'm* going to find your pearl?" asked Tommy, forgetting he was supposed to be a great wizard.

"Why, Mr. Tuddleby, I'm surprised. I thought you said . . ."

"I meant *of course* I'm going to find your pearl," Tommy quickly corrected himself.

"Yes indeed!" piped up Horatio. "Now come along."

"Where are we going?"

"To see Queen Violet and her brother, Prince Alexander."

"Oh!" Tommy gasped. "I've never met a queen or a prince before."

"You must be very respectful and obedient when in their presence. They have had a most troubling time. Their father, King Tintoretto, died not long ago. And with the pearl missing . . ." Horatio sighed.

"At least the prince is back," noted Olly.

"Where was he?" Tommy asked, growing confused with all the names and events.

Olly turned to Horatio. "I heard he was rebuilding the old garrison north of Tacitonia—is that right? Anyway, it's been many months . . . almost a year, I think. He just returned . . ." Olly paused, frowning. "What will happen, Sir Horatio? I mean, who will rule?"

"Isn't it the person who's oldest that rules?" questioned Tommy, looking from one man to the other.

"Not if they're twins," replied Horatio. "Which they are. In which case the king chooses his successor. With the prince away so much, he chose Violet. I'm not sure why that would change. In any case, until we find the pearl, things will remain the same. The queen is so happy to have Alexander home again, but she'll be even more pleased when she sees Mr. Tuddleby. So let's push on. We haven't any time to lose."

The Dream Ends

H ey! Look at all the water!" Tommy exclaimed as they approached the palace. "I always read about moats in books, but it's for real."

"This palace was built hundreds of years ago," Horatio informed him as they crossed the wide stone bridge. Two enormous gates, decorated with statues and intricate designs, blocked their path.

"You can't tell under these circumstances, but our new queen lives in the most beautiful palace ever built!" Olly said grandly.

"Ah, here we are! Let me announce our arrival," Horatio declared.

Horatio approached the two gate guards, who wore matching dark gray jackets with silver buttons from bottom to top, black pants, hats with feathers, and high black boots. He spoke a few words. They nodded and heaved open the gates.

Inside, Tommy, Olly and Horatio passed gardens and small houses, which, Horatio explained, were where the palace workers lived with their families. Another guard approached and led them through a smaller gate.

Tommy's eyes sparkled with excitement. "The palace. It *is* beautiful . . . even without color!"

Indeed, the palace stood grand and magnificent as any fairy-tale castle, lit by hundreds of torches set into crystal holders on the glistening white stone walls and atop the numerous turrets and steeples. Carved ornaments adorned each turret, and a flag waved from the pointed roofs. Imposing sculptures of enormous, lionlike creatures stood on each side of the entryway, and the wall above it displayed four large, painted scenes from the story of the Pearls of Colloster. Even in shades of gray, the detail of each picture was exquisite.

As they passed through the entryway, Tommy saw that the castle walls were not smooth at all but rather made of small, sparkling seashells and pieces of sea glass. Inside, the floor was covered by a thick carpet of very fine grains of powdery white sand. A servant led them into a small parlor and handed them cool, damp cloths to wipe their faces. When they were done, they sat on a soft, silky couch. Tommy nestled his head against a velvet pillow and sighed with relief. The air here was much more comfortable than outside.

It wasn't long before a young woman swept into the room. She was dressed in a long summer gown that flowed to the floor, and her thick, dark hair, nearly as long, fell in waves around her. The beauty of her warm, dark eyes and delicate features was shadowed with sleeplessness and worry.

"The pearl," she cried. "Oh, Sir Horatio, the pearl of Tacitonia. They think it has been stolen!"

"What?!" Horatio and Olly exclaimed at once, jumping to their feet. Tommy quickly did the same.

"It's true, Sir Horatio," she responded breathlessly. "Alexander has left already." She stopped suddenly, noticing Tommy for the first time. "I'm so sorry. You must be Thomas Tuddleby."

Horatio nudged Tommy, and he bowed as low as he could, almost losing his balance. As he did so, he noticed that her gown was covered in butterfly-like creatures, some of which had fluttered to the floor and seemed to be lifting the hem of her gown so it wouldn't catch in her sandals.

"Are you the queen?" asked Tommy.

The woman smiled weakly. "Yes, and as you can see, we need your help desperately."

"Please, Queen Violet, tell us what has happened," urged Horatio.

She sat down on a grand chair and gestured for them to return to the couch. "A messenger came shortly after you left," she explained. "He said the pearl in Tacitonia was missing."

"So you're not *sure* it was stolen," corrected Horatio.

"No," she admitted, "but Alexander thought it would be best to go there immediately."

"He should have waited for me to return."

"There wasn't time. What if someone *is* stealing the pearls?"

"Then that means I didn't just lose our pearl!" Olly burst out. He looked at Tommy. "But if that's so, do you think you'll be able to find it now?"

"Yes," echoed Queen Violet, "can you find our pearl?"

"I . . . I . . ." stammered Tommy. He was saved from answering when an older woman entered, carrying a tray of small ash-colored sandwiches and a teapot.

"Thank you, Temma," Queen Violet said kindly, nodding at the woman. "That will be all for now."

Horatio poured a muddy gray liquid into four cups. "Obviously, with such news, the plans must change."

"How so?" asked Olly, biting hungrily into a sandwich. He appeared to be feeling much better. He looked over at Tommy, who had not touched any of his food or drink, and whispered, "I know it all looks quite unappetizing, Mr. Tuddleby, but I assure you it is delicious. Just close your eyes. You'll see." He moved the cup closer to Tommy and placed a sandwich on a plate for him.

"We must go to Tacitonia," declared Horatio.

"Where's that?" asked Tommy, taking a very small sip from his cup. It tasted like spiced apple cider. He then bit into the sandwich, which tasted like chicken salad.

"The neighboring land."

"But the prince is already there."

"And that's why we must go. If the pearl has been misplaced, we'll know soon enough. But if it has been stolen, he may need our help."

"But, Sir Horatio," protested Queen Violet, "Alexander gave specific instructions for you to remain here until he sends word."

The little man shook his head. "We would be poor subjects if we left our prince to face such problems alone."

"I thought we were supposed to be obedient," piped up Tommy.

"We would do little good *here* if the pearl stealer is in Tacitonia," the little man retorted.

Violet sighed softly. "Will you need anyone else to accompany you besides our wayfaring wizard?"

Again, Horatio shook his head.

Olly looked dismally at them all. "My one chance for a true adventure, and I must remain here?"

"I don't see why you should." Tommy looked at Horatio. "Isn't he coming?"

"I hadn't planned . . ."

"But *color* is missing, and it only makes sense to take the color guard with us."

"Yes, yes! Of course!" Olly brightened. "And I can do innumerable things. After all, I wanted to be an adventurer for years and years before I was the color guard. I read lots of books. I know I could be useful."

"And it's your duty," Tommy asserted.

"Of course it's my duty." Olly nodded vigorously.

Horatio threw up his hands. "Enough! You've convinced me. Now we have to prepare ourselves."

"When will we leave?" asked Tommy.

"By dawn tomorrow." Horatio glanced at his pocket watch. "But now it's late. Tommy, Olly, I suggest you retire after dinner. I will arrange supplies for our journey."

WHEN THEY HAD FINISHED EATING, TEMMA RETURNED and led Tommy and Olly into the sleeping quarters.

"Wow. This has been a most amazing dream," Tommy said under his breath. "What did you say?" asked Olly.

"Oh, I didn't think you would hear me. In fact, I wasn't sure if you could. When you're part of the dream, I mean," replied Tommy, stumbling over his words. "I mean, I wasn't sure if people in a dream can hear me talk about the dream."

"What in the world are you talking about, Mr. Tuddleby?" Olly said, confused.

"Nothing," said Tommy. "Good night. See you tomorrow . . . maybe . . . probably not, actually . . ." Tommy trailed off. But Olly now looked thoroughly alarmed, so he quickly added, "Just kidding, Olly."

"Oh!" Olly said, much relieved. "Of course. Of course!" He disappeared into his room, saying, "Good night, Mr. Tuddleby!"

"Good night!" Tommy called after him.

Tommy let out his breath as the door closed. *That was a close one.* He changed into the cotton pajamas Temma had given to him and snuggled under the covers of a huge feather bed. "Goodbye, dream," he said sadly. He tried to stay awake and make the dream last, but he dropped almost immediately into a deep sleep.

EARLY THE NEXT MORNING—SO EARLY, IN FACT, THAT THE moons still lit the dusky sky—a hand shook Tommy's shoulder. He blinked awake, his eyes widening as he saw first Temma and then a set of sturdy traveling clothes neatly draped over the back of a chair.

"What?!" exclaimed Tommy. "I'm still here?"

Temma looked at him, confused. "Mr. Tuddleby? Are you all right? Of course you're here. Where else would you be?"

"I thought I was dreaming," replied Tommy slowly. "But this is real!" He felt surprisingly calm, given that he had no idea how to get home . . . or if he even could get home—what if he was in a different universe? Now he was pretty excited at the prospect of solving this mystery. No more playacting. This land was in trouble, and they were depending on him. He felt so . . . important.

"You're not making any sense, Mr. Tuddleby," said Temma. "But you must hurry. Sir Horatio is very anxious to leave."

"Right!" Tommy jumped out of bed, feeling energized. His new pants were much nicer than the ones he usually wore, and he'd been given a black jacket to go over a crinkly cotton shirt. Gazing at himself in a mirror, he thought he looked pretty good. Very . . . grown up. But something wasn't quite right. He replaced the jacket with his old brown one and took another look. Much better. Both sharp *and* ready for action. Like Jake Jones.

He grabbed his satchel and scurried down the palace stairs in search of Horatio and Olly.

Tommy wandered in and out of several enormous rooms before he bumped into Temma again. She directed him to the breakfast room and told him to eat as much as he liked from what remained on the table while he waited for the others.

The rising sun, hidden behind dark clouds, barely brightened the room when Tommy finally found it. At the center stood a large, rectangular wooden table, covered with the remains of a recent, hurried breakfast. One platter held what looked like buttered pancakes, still warm, with some kind of berries and a sticky sweet syrup dribbled on top. Like everything else, it was a smudgy gray color. Recalling the previous night, Tommy filled a plate, closed his eyes, breathed in the delectable smells, and began to eat, imagining golden-brown pancakes, amber syrup, and dark-purple berries.

He hadn't yet finished when he heard Horatio's voice. "There you are, Mr. Tuddleby," puffed the little man as he and Olly entered the room. "I'm glad you've already eaten." He patted Tommy's arm. "It's time we go."

Tommy inhaled the rest of his breakfast as they rushed to finish collecting maps and parcels of food. Horatio had found a belt long enough to fit around his waist. When everything was done, they went to say their goodbyes.

Queen Violet smiled at Tommy as she said, "Thank you for agreeing to help my people." Then she kissed each of them on the forehead. "When you find Alexander, give him my good wishes. Remember, there are friends of the kingdom all around. They will provide help when you are in need. Good luck. I pray for your great success."

OUTSIDE THE PALACE, AN OPPRESSIVE HEAT BEAT DOWN ON them, even worse than the day before. Olly, Horatio, and Tommy trudged for several miles to the bridge over the Collos. Beyond it, the wide road led to the forest.

From what Tommy could see, the forest was very dark and grim. The boughs of tall trees formed an arc over their path, blocking even more of the already dim light.

"Without color it certainly looks gloomy," Tommy remarked.

"The forests used to be harmless," said Horatio. "But ever since the pearl has been missing, they've grown dark and eerie."

"There isn't any other way to go?" Olly asked.

"Unfortunately, no," said Horatio, shuffling all of his packages into the crook of one arm. "We need to pick up our supplies from Caleb's place on the other side of the forest. We could go around it, but that would add an extra day to our trip, and we simply haven't the time. Do you have those torches?" he said, turning to Olly.

"Torches?" Olly replied, puzzled.

Horatio stopped in his tracks. "Olly, you do have the torches . . . don't you?"

"Uh . . ."

"In the bag I asked you to take?"

"Bag?" said Olly meekly.

Horatio groaned. "I'm not sure we'll be able to find the forest path if we don't have any light."

"Maybe Mr. Tuddleby can use his magic?" Olly suggested hopefully.

"Of course," exclaimed Horatio. "This *is* such a small thing. You must be able to do *some*thing."

Tommy opened his mouth, about to say, "Not really," but then he remembered: the illuminating wand! This was his chance to show a little wizard magic.

"No problem!" Tommy said. He retrieved the wand and flicked it once, declaring, "Alitium!" and pressing the button on its handle at the same time. The tip of the wand glowed white. "This should brighten our way so we don't get lost," said Tommy triumphantly.

"Well done, Mr. Tuddleby!" said Olly.

"Indeed!" said Horatio, much relieved. "But even with this light, we must be careful," he added. "We've heard stories of animals appearing during the day that used to only come out at night. Some of them can be quite dangerous. Especially the tree spiders."

"What?" exclaimed Olly and Tommy simultaneously.

"The spiders. They are small—not even an inch long—but quite venomous, and their webs are fine but strong as thick rope. So watch out."

Tommy took a deep breath and nodded. "All right, then. Let's go."

As they walked deeper into the woods, a strong, earthy smell permeated the air, which had cooled somewhat and was now at least bearable. Tommy could barely see the gnarled tree trunks, even with his wand.

As the path curved past a very odd-looking tree with a straight upper trunk and a lower trunk that looked like the letter *S*, Tommy whispered, "That's so cool, don't you think?"

There was no response.

"Olly? Horatio?" He stopped and looked back. His companions were nowhere to be seen.

The Wolf, the Web, and the Wizard

Tommy retraced his steps slowly and quietly, hoping nothing that might find him appetizing would notice he was alone. Out of the corner of his eye, he saw a pair of gray saucer eyes: an animal the size of a large raccoon was staring out at him. He looked away to discourage it from coming any closer.

Suddenly Olly's voice pierced the silence: "Help! Help! Mr. Tuddleby! Save us!"

Tommy ran toward the voice.

"Over there! Sir Horatio!" he heard from above. He looked up, and there was Olly, clinging to a branch high up in a tree and pointing to something. "There!" he shrieked. "Please hurry!" Tommy turned, and there, in the dark, he could barely see Horatio tangled in something, his head slumped over. Then he heard a deep growl. Tommy held his wand out. The light revealed a large, wolflike creature slowly approaching Horatio.

Tommy dug frantically through his satchel, muttering, "Where is it, where is it? Come on! Ah yes!" He pulled out his survival whistle. He wasn't sure if these creatures were anything like the wolves back home, but when he and his dad went camping, Dad always told him that wolves are really more afraid of you than you are of them and if you stand up tall, stare straight into their eyes, and make a lot of noise, they usually run away. He could only hope Aesteron wolves were no different.

"Use your magic!" Olly pleaded. The creature was now just a few feet from Horatio.

Tommy stood up as tall as he could, stuck out his wand, and waved it around, shouting the joke his friends had loved to tell when they were little: "Owa Tagoo Siam. Owa Tagoo Siam. Owa. Tagoo. Siam." Then he blew the whistle, which let out an ear-piercing blast. He chanted some more at the top of his voice before blowing the whistle again. The creature stopped moving toward Horatio but then turned to Tommy with a glare. Tommy raised both of his arms as high as he could, pointed his wand at it, and stared back, not blinking. After a few long seconds, the creature turned and ran into the woods.

Tommy rushed toward the little man, calling, "Horatio, are you okay?"

"That was amazing," shouted Olly as he slid down the tree trunk to the ground. He sprinted toward them.

Horatio looked stunned. "What? What happened?" He looked from Olly to Tommy.

"You fainted, Sir Horatio!" said Olly, and he gave Horatio a very brief summary of how Tommy had faced down the creature.

"Thank goodness," Horatio murmured. "Thank you, Mr. Tuddleby. What would we do without you?"

"No problem," Tommy said as calmly as he could, even though he thought nothing of the sort. In the darkness, they couldn't see that Tommy was shaking all over. He had never been so scared in all his life. He let out a deep breath.

"How am I going to get out of this?" asked Horatio worriedly. "I'm completely stuck!"

Tommy shined his wand upward and saw that Horatio's body was snagged in a thick, sticky spider's web. "How did this happen?"

"It's my fault," Olly said, sounding guilty. "I saw the most interesting mushrooms growing behind a rock and paused to take a look. Just then we heard a sound. We thought it was you, Mr. Tuddleby, coming back toward us, but instead we saw that terrible creature!"

"I instructed Olly to climb up a tree," continued Horatio, "but I'm not quite so . . . nimble as Olly, and in trying to find a tree that I could climb, I backed straight into the web and got caught in it. I couldn't move an inch. The creature moved toward me, and that's when I—"

"—fainted," interrupted Olly. "And that's when I yelled for you, Mr. Tuddleby!"

"Tommy. It's time both of you called me Tommy," corrected Tommy. "Well, let's see if I have something to get you out of this."

"What about one of your spells?"

Tommy looked up. "Uh . . . it's a wizard's . . . uh . . . wizard's vow . . . not to use magic unless absolutely necessary. And it just so happens no magic is needed here!" He dug into his satchel once more, removed the pocket knife, and displayed it in the palm of his hand. He poked the wand's glowing tip at the web to figure out where best to cut. With the help of Olly—who was much stronger than he appeared—Tommy sliced into the web and began to pull it apart.

Just then Olly drew in a sharp breath. Tommy glanced over at him. Olly jerked his head at a part of the web above them and whispered, "Hurry!" Several small, hairy black spiders with thick legs and pincers were crawling toward Horatio's head.

Horatio looked from Olly to Tommy. "What? What's the matter?"

Olly grabbed the knife and made several quick cuts into the web, and together Olly and Tommy pulled the last of the strands off of Horatio and yanked him to the ground.

"Oof!" Horatio exclaimed, rubbing his shoulder. "What was all that about?"

"Thank goodness!" Olly heaved a sigh of relief. He held out a hand and pulled Horatio to his feet.

Tommy pointed his wand again toward the web, which was now covered with spiders. Horatio's face paled. "Goodness indeed."

"Come, Sir Horatio," Olly said gently. "We must move on." Horatio nodded as Tommy worked to rid Horatio's clothes of the gummy strands.

Guided by the wand, they found their way back to the forest path. Twigs snapped all around them, and the chirps and screeches and howls of unknown creatures grew louder and nearer. Soon, however, they saw a gleam of light and hurried to leave the thickest region of the forest behind.

"That was a close call!" Tommy remarked with a final shudder as they stepped onto a brighter road. He inspected his hand and peeled off a thick strand of web, which he shoved into his left pants pocket as a sort of souvenir.

"We shouldn't have any problems traveling through the rest of the forest," said Horatio, who seemed to have mostly recovered. "And we should be reaching Caleb's place soon."

THE AIR GREW EVEN COLDER AS THEY APPROACHED THE forest's edge. Olly didn't seem to notice. He was too busy rushing from tree to tree, examining each with excitement. "Over here is a berribi, and over there is a rodinia, and to the right is a pyrus dentata tree. You find all sorts of wild fruit, nuts, and berries in the forest. Some you can eat and some you can't. And *I* know which are which," he boasted.

"Wow, that's pretty good," Tommy exclaimed.

"Indeed," Horatio agreed. "We can certainly use such knowledge as we travel."

"I'm *more* than a color guard, you know," Olly added, and Horatio and Tommy smiled at each other.

As the sun fell lower in the sky, the temperature dropped even further. They sped up and soon reached a small village in a large clearing. In the center stood a stable and a large stone building with a front-door sign informing them that they had reached Caleb's Border House.

Outside, a girl was fixing a wagon. Like Tommy— and unlike everyone and everything else around her—she was in full color, wearing a red-and-blue long-sleeved jersey, blue overalls, and a red-and-blue-checkered cloth headband that kept her unruly hair away from her face. Her overalls were covered in pockets, and a tiny hand poked out of each. As Tommy watched, she tapped a pocket and opened her hand, and the little hand disappeared into the pocket and then reappeared with a small pair of pliers. She

41

tightened a bolt and then handed the tool back to the little hand, which grabbed it and then dropped it inside the pocket again.

The girl looked to be a little older than Tommy. She saw the trio, wiped the sweat from her forehead, and raised her eyebrows in a questioning manner.

"We're looking for Caleb," said Horatio. "Can you please tell him Sir Horatio Hue is here?"

Without a word, the girl ran into the supply house. A moment later she reappeared, accompanied by a huge, muscular man. He towered over them, broad-shouldered and tall, with dark, bushy eyebrows, a thick salt-and-pepper beard, and hair to match. Like the girl, he wore overalls covered in pockets and a striped shirt underneath, but all in shades of gray.

"Sir Horatio! Olly!" He grabbed Horatio's hand and shook it heartily. "And you must be the famous Mr. Tuddleby," he boomed, turning to Tommy. Tommy shook Caleb's hand as firmly as he could.

"Well, no need to be waiting outside," exclaimed Caleb. "Come in. Come in." He hustled them inside. The girl followed.

The room they entered was small and sparsely furnished but very cozy. The travelers plopped down on the soft blankets that littered the floor and warmed themselves by the crackling fire.

Caleb turned to the girl and said, "Raia, please fetch four mugs of my razmus brew. And one for yourself if you'd like." She nodded and disappeared into another room.

"No problems in the forest, I hope?" inquired Caleb, taking a seat.

Tommy felt the sticky web in his pocket and smiled to himself while Horatio told Caleb of their adventures. The tall man shook his head. "It's dangerous to travel nowadays. Strange things have been happening lately, ever since our color . . ." He rose. "But you're here for your provisions. Let me check on them."

No sooner had he left than Raia entered the room, carrying four steaming mugs of what looked like hot cocoa. The welcoming smell raised their spirits, and one sweet sip melted the numbness in their toes.

When Caleb returned, he assured them everything was ready but insisted they stay the night. "It's getting mighty cold out there. Never used to be. Least not at these times. But the last couple of days it's been that way. Weather's gone bad—terrible storms and flooding."

"I thought it seemed awfully cold out while we were walking," remarked Tommy.

Caleb shook his head again. "Sure'd like to know what's going on."

Horatio nodded grimly. "That's what we'd like to know. Have you heard anything about Tacitonia? Did they find their pearl?"

"No, it's still missing. And the people there when it went missing, like my niece"—he nodded toward Raia— "can't speak a whisper. In fact there are no sounds at all – not from birds, or the river, or even a door slamming shut. Nothing!"

"What?!" the three visitors cried in disbelief. They all turned to Raia. "What happened?"

She shrugged her shoulders.

"It's been a bit challenging to communicate," Caleb said apologetically, "but from what I could figure out, Raia was going through the town square in Tacitonia to her mother's house yesterday when she heard all this ruckus, and—"

"Excuse me, Mr. Caleb," interrupted Olly, "I might be—"

"Shh, Olly," said Horatio. "Let Caleb finish."

"But you see—"

"Olly!" chided Horatio. "Go on, Caleb."

"Well, two of the town leaders were yelling about the pearl. Each one was saying the other had lost it. But no one thought much of it because it's happened before."

Tommy grinned at Olly. "See, Olly, you're not the only one."

The color guard blushed.

"Anyway," continued Caleb, "this morning I went back to see if my sister, who has been ill, was doing any better, and to fetch Raia—she's been helping me out these

44

last few months—but nothing was the same! They tried to talk, all right, but no sounds came out. Same with everyone and everything else!"

Horatio looked at Olly. Olly looked at Tommy. And Tommy didn't know what to do, so he looked at his wriggling toes. A land of no color. A land of no sound. More and more, it seemed the disappearance of the two pearls was no coincidence.

"Did you see the prince there?" asked Horatio.

"Who?"

"Alexander."

"You mean the prince of Aesteron? Why'd he be in Tacitonia?"

"He wanted to find out about the pearl."

Caleb shook his head. "I didn't see the prince—course, I've never seen him, so I don't know what he looks like—but imagine . . ." Then, as if he'd broken from a trance, he abruptly turned to Raia. "You should finish your chores. It's getting late."

Raia nodded and left.

"If the pearl's been stolen," said Olly after a short silence, "the prince is probably chasing after the person who took it, don't you think, Sir Horatio?"

"You're probably right," Horatio replied, "which means we should leave as soon as possible."

"Well, everything's ready for the morning," said Caleb. "But now you better sleep. It's no good traveling at this time of night." They all rose stiffly to their feet and followed Caleb, who opened a door and said, "Olly and Sir Horatio, you'll be staying here." Then he led Tommy down the hall to another door. "Mr. Tuddleby, you'll be staying here."

"My own room? That's really nice of you, Mr. Caleb."

"Well, you are the magician who's going to save us! So it seems only proper. I assume you have some planning to do and could use some peace and quiet."

"Ah, sure," Tommy said. "It *is* a very big problem." He took a deep breath. "I just hope I can figure it out."

"I'm sure you will, Mr. Tuddleby," said Caleb encouragingly. "I'm sure you will." The door clicked shut behind him as he left.

"I hope so," Tommy said to himself. Now that he knew this wasn't a dream, he had to figure things out. For real.

The Plot Thickens

The next morning, Caleb's cook served up a breakfast of meat slices, thick doughy pastries, and a bubbling hot cereal sweetened with syrup. By now Tommy had gotten used to the gray color of everything and didn't even have to close his eyes to imagine how good it must really look before taking his first bite. While they were eating, Raia entered the room, wearing a jacket and holding a travel bag. Caleb looked up, surprised.

"Raia?"

She pointed at herself and then at Tommy, Horatio, and Olly.

"No, Raia," said Caleb sternly. "Put your things away. You're staying here."

Raia found a notepad and a pen and scribbled, "My city. My voice. I want to help!"

"Raia, it's not your place."

Raia shook her head. "No!" she wrote. "I go with them. Or on my own."

"Raia. We've talked about this!" Caleb turned toward the travelers. "Ever since my niece discovered Mr. Tuddleby was stopping here, she's insisted she join you in the search." He turned back to Raia. "I'm sorry, Raia. You'll just be in the way. Go do your chores."

Angry tears streamed down Raia's face. She wiped them away and stomped out of the room. Caleb shook his head.

"I'm sorry, Sir Horatio. I've been telling her not to interfere. But she's a stubborn one. Even without a voice!"

"No worries, Caleb," Horatio said kindly. "Everyone is upset. Don't be too hard on her."

Caleb nodded. "Thank you for understanding." He motioned to the door. "Time to get you saddled up!"

Caleb took them to the stables and led out three animals that seemed to be part donkey and part horse—mulions. "Mew-lee-ons," as Caleb pronounced them, were the work animals used by farmers for hauling and plowing. They were good and strong companions for any long journey.

The mulions were well groomed with sleek, dark coats. Their muzzles were white, and a white ring surrounded each eye. Their faces seemed to smile, although their gentle, innocent eyes looked sad. Their legs, thick and strong, were short in relation to their large bodies, and shaggy white hair fringed the lower part of each leg.

Tommy ran over to a mulion with one white ear and one gray ear and stroked its flank. "Gosh, they're beautiful, Caleb! Can this one be mine?"

"Sure thing, Mr. Tuddleby. I figured you'd like that one. Her name is Kia."

Olly stared at the animals and then at Caleb. "They seem rather small. Will they be able to carry us in addition to our baggage and food?"

"Oh, yes," Caleb promised. "They're very strong. We use them to do all our hard labor, and they can travel miles before getting tired. But mulions are good in other ways too. They can nose out anything that might be dangerous, and they know their enemies from their friends. They never get lost, and they'll *never* leave your side."

"*Sounds* good," Olly said with little conviction.

"They're great!" Tommy exclaimed, and wrapping his arms around his mulion's neck, he gave her a big kiss on the tip of her moist nose.

Horatio raised his eyebrows at Tommy. "Really?"

Tommy stepped back and blushed, realizing he'd forgotten he was supposed to be a lot older than he looked. "They're just so . . . uh . . . cute," he said in as deep a voice as he could muster.

"Evidently," Horatio replied wryly.

When they had gathered their supplies—blankets, rope, food parcels, cooking utensils, and other useful tools—each of the travelers mounted a mulion. Olly was very nervous sitting on his. He slipped and slid every time it took a step and jumped every time it uttered its high-pitched bray. But once he was able to control it, they were ready to be on their way. Caleb wished them a safe journey and told them the shortest route to Tacitonia. As long as they followed the river, he said, they would never be lost.

THEY HAD RIDDEN FOR MOST OF THE DAY WHEN TOMMY brought his mulion to a sudden stop and pointed to the sky. "Look over there! Isn't it beautiful? Color's back!"

They all stopped, captivated by a breathtaking sunset where crimson and blue lights mingled with layers of marshmallow clouds.

"It *is* a wonderful sight to see," Horatio agreed. "We must be very near Tacitonia."

They guided the mulions along the main road, which was bordered by the last scatterings of forest trees. But no sooner did the sun disappear and the moons come out than the temperature dropped sharply and deep rumblings sounded in the distance. One icy droplet of water fell from above and then another and another.

"I'm getting cold and wet," complained Olly. "And is that thunder? What a horrible racket!"

Tommy turned to Horatio. "It *is* getting awful out here. Are we almost at the border?"

"Yes, Tommy," Horatio replied. "And Klaton, the city where the pearl is, lies nearby. I'm sure we can stay there tonight. Who would leave us out in the cold and rain?"

The moment they crossed the river and passed the sign welcoming them into Tacitonia, two things changed. First, the grass turned red. In fact, everything was a different color than Tommy had expected to see. Trees had green bark and yellow leaves. Flowers had blue stems. Also, to their astonishment, the sounds of groaning thunder ceased. In fact, there were no sounds at all except for the clipping of the mulions' hooves. The rain fell, and every so often a streak of bright green lightning shimmered against the clouded skies. Horatio and Olly looked so sad and gray surrounded by all of the color. And without all the familiar sounds in the background, it was rather lonely.

When they entered the main street of Klaton, several people ran out of their homes to greet them. The peoples' mouths moved, but not a word was uttered. When Horatio spoke, however, no one could help but listen to him. His was the only voice to be heard for miles and miles. He explained to them that he, Olly, and Tommy had come to find the pearl. The people looked distrustfully at the newcomers, blocking the mulions from moving either forward or backward.

"We're here to help you," insisted Tommy. No one stirred. "It's storming out. At least let us stay the night."

The people exchanged uncertain glances until one woman brushed their worries aside. She showed the visitors where they could tie up the mulions and then beckoned them into the town hall. Inside, several small groups of adults and children huddled together.

Horatio's voice broke the silence. "We must speak to the pearl guard. Could anyone tell us who—"

The woman who had ushered them in stepped forward.

"Is it you?"

She nodded.

"What happened to the pearl? Why can no one speak?"

She tried to explain, but Horatio exhaled in frustration. "However are we going to understand? Does anyone have a pen and paper?" He turned to Tommy. "Or perhaps you have magic that—"

"She says the pearl is missing. That's why there's no sound here," interjected Olly.

Horatio stared up at Olly, astounded. "How . . . how did you know what she said?"

"I can read lips." Olly shrugged. "I tried to tell you at Caleb's, Sir Horatio, but you just kept shushing me!"

Olly turned to the woman. "I'm not very good at it, but when I wanted to become an adventurer, I used to read about all these different places I could go to, and one of them—"

"Never mind the explanations," Tommy interrupted. "If you can do it, then what are we waiting for?"

Olly told the woman what Caleb had described to them. She began speaking very animatedly. When she finally paused, Olly turned to Tommy and Horatio.

"The pearl guard's name is Tirzah. Everything Raia told us about the pearl is true. They're not sure how it was stolen. At first she thought she had only mislaid it, but she couldn't find it even after searching everywhere."

"We haven't been able to find the pearl in Rolokon either," Horatio informed her.

She signaled to Olly.

"Tirzah wants to know why anyone would do such a thing," he said.

Horatio grimly shook his head. "That is what we are trying to find out. But please, you must tell us everything that has happened."

Olly watched her closely and then continued. "She says that during the past two days, as soon as the sun sets, it grows bitterly cold. Rain falls in torrents, the river floods, and a fierce wind blows. Lightning causes many trees to fall. The people are sure demons and witches rule the night. She says it's not safe to be out alone.

"The flooding and winds are destroying their houses. Yet during the day, the sun shines. And there's silence. Nothing makes a noise, not even the crickets at night."

"Then why can we speak aloud and no one else can? After all, we're in the land," commented Tommy.

"Tirzah says this silence seems to apply only to what was in the land at the time the pearl was stolen. Sometimes, she says, you can hear the sounds of those that weren't here at the time, such as us, or a wild animal, or a single clap of thunder from a visiting cloud."

"How funny," murmured Tommy. "But I guess that makes sense. I mean, Raia and I were the only ones in Rolokon with any color, and now Olly and Horatio are the only ones here without it."

"It doesn't seem at all funny to me," said Olly. "In fact, it seems quite serious. Think how dangerous it must be to travel at night."

Horatio frowned. "We'll soon find that out for ourselves. The next stretch of road runs for miles on end, and I doubt we'll find an inn."

Olly gulped. "What do you mean? Aren't we returning to the palace?"

"Our job is to find these pearls, Olly. The more I hear, the more sure I am something is terribly wrong. It's unlikely that two pearls could be misplaced within days of each other. In other words—"

"—in other words, someone *is* stealing them," Tommy interrupted excitedly, "which means we have to reach the next land before the thief strikes again!"

Horatio glanced up at Tommy and nodded. "Indeed, if . . . *if* the pearls are being stolen, that is exactly what we must do."

Horatio turned to Tirzah. "Have you seen another gentleman around these parts? He must have asked for shelter, for he is a traveler like us. He came here to help search for your pearl."

Tirzah shook her head.

"But where could the prince be?" asked Olly anxiously.

Tirzah only shrugged her shoulders.

"I knew he shouldn't have traveled alone," muttered Horatio. "What if he's not safe?" He punched his fist into the palm of his hand. "Don't you see?" He looked up wearily, almost painfully. "It is my responsibility . . ."

"Perhaps he discovered who the pearl stealer was before he even reached the village. Maybe he's following another road," suggested Tommy.

They were all dissatisfied with this explanation, but after asking a few more questions about the pearl, they found there was no more to be learned. The travelers ended their investigations with a light meal of bread and broth, and then retired for the evening at a nearby inn. But strangely enough, the eerie silence kept them awake for some time. It was *too* quiet and far from comforting.

THE NEXT MORNING, THEY AWOKE AND WENT OUTSIDE. A warm summer sun blazed fiery rays upon their tired faces. They could see the gushing of draining rainwater and feel the moist soil beneath their feet, but they heard nothing.

Tommy gazed at the dazzling scenery. "I can't believe that only last night it was so miserable outside."

Tirzah nodded and wrote down her final warning. "Do not forget last night. It will happen again tonight."

"Must we go on?" whimpered Olly.

"Yes, Olly," Horatio replied firmly. "How else are we going to help the people of Tacitonia? And who knows what will happen to the rest of the lands if we don't capture the pearl thief or at least find out what is happening to the kingdom?"

So they packed their belongings, mounted the mulions, and bid the silent people goodbye.

THE DIRT ROAD THEY FOLLOWED CLIMBED HIGHER AND higher, twisting around hills. Because of the storm, the road was flooded in parts and littered with the fallen branches of surrounding trees. With every step, the mulions' hooves sank into the ground. Finally, Tommy and his friends decided it would be best to dismount and walk. They took turns leading the way.

At midafternoon it was Olly and his mulion who walked ahead—until, that is, he disappeared around a curve. The ground beneath their feet suddenly shook, and Tommy and Horatio heard a shout and a mulion's whinny. They hurried around the corner. Just a few feet ahead to their left, a fast-moving river of soil and debris cascaded down the hillside, flooded the roadway, and flowed down a steep ravine on the other side toward the river. Olly's mulion stood at the edge of the ravine, just beyond the mudflow. Olly, however, was nowhere to be seen. The mulion had sensed the danger ahead. Olly had not.

"Olly!" Tommy yelled. "Olly, where are you?"

Tommy thought he heard a faint "Help" from the ravine. He and Horatio exchanged glances.

"Olly!" Tommy rushed toward the edge of the ravine, but his feet slipped out from under him. He too would have been carried over the side by the flowing mud, had Horatio not hooked his cane around the collar of Tommy's jacket and pulled him back.

"No, Tommy! It's too dangerous." He looked up the hillside to where the mudslide had started. Already the mudflow had slowed. "This won't last much longer. We need to wait for it to stop."

"But . . ."

"No!" Horatio said sternly. "You nearly got yourself killed with that last antic. Do you have any spell to stop this? If so, be my guest."

"No . . . I mean . . . yes . . . I mean . . ."

"Tommy! Sir Horatio! Help me! Please!"

The mud had nearly stopped flowing, so Horatio and Tommy stepped closer to the edge of the ravine. Several feet below they saw Olly, clutching the branch of a tall tree, his legs swinging wildly to and fro.

"Olly," called Horatio, "stop thrashing about! Try to loop your legs around the branch."

"I can't! I'm going to fall!"

The tree branch was just far enough away that Tommy and Horatio could not reach him. Tommy thought that Olly might be able to jump down instead, but then he saw, just beyond the trunk, a steep drop toward the rushing waters of the Collos.

Just then, they heard a sound—footsteps and the clopping of hooves!—racing toward them.

Tommy spun around, his eyes widening in surprise.

The Tuddleby Trait

Raia! What are *you* doing here?"

In a matter of seconds, Raia removed a thick coil of rope from her mulion's saddle, secured the rope around a nearby tree trunk, and edged her way to the ravine until she was as near as she could safely be to where Olly was floundering. Then she whipped the free end of the rope over her head and flung it toward Olly's branch. It slapped down right in front of Olly, who seized it and pulled himself up the side of the ravine.

"Raia!" Olly exclaimed. "Thank you! I was sure I was going to *die*. You saved my life!"

Raia blushed.

"Don't exaggerate, Olly," chided Tommy. "You weren't going to die."

"Well, that's what you think," Olly replied indignantly. "I could have fallen right into the river and washed away. Why didn't you use your magician powers to save me?"

"I was about to," protested Tommy. "But then Raia showed up and had it under control before I had a chance to finish!"

"Yes, but—"

"Enough!" interrupted Horatio. "Raia, how did you get here? *Why* are you here?"

Raia answered, but there was only silence. She shook her head.

"Right," said Horatio. He turned to Olly, who was cleaning himself off as best as he could. "We need your assistance."

Raia repeated her response to Olly, motioning to Horatio and Tommy.

"Raia says she's here to help us find the pearl thief. Apparently she's been following us since we left Tacitonia."

"No, no, no," said Horatio, shaking his head. "This will not do. You need to go back to your uncle. Does he even know where you are?"

Raia shook her head and spoke to Olly for a few minutes before he related her story.

60

"Raia told her uncle she wanted to look after her mother until the pearl was found. She left shortly after we did, and when she arrived in Tacitonia, she saw us speaking to Tirzah. When we headed to the inn, she went to her mother's for the night. She left very early, telling her mother she was returning to work at Caleb's. So it appears no one knows she's missing."

"This will not do, Raia! Things could get dangerous!"

Raia gave a fierce look, stamped her foot, and mouthed, "Not leaving," so clearly even Tommy and Horatio could understand.

"Sir Horatio, I think we should let her stay," said Olly. "She saved my life, after all!"

"Olly, she did not save your life!" objected Tommy. "Anyone could have done that!"

Raia stamped her foot again in frustration.

"Raia says she's traveled all over this kingdom with her mother and she could be helpful in making sure we don't get lost, or maybe even finding shortcuts to where we need to go."

Raia looked pleadingly from Horatio to Tommy. "Please," she mouthed.

Tommy gazed down at his shoes. *If she comes along,* he thought, *she might figure out my secret, and if she tells Horatio and Olly, they'll be upset and Horatio might send me back.* She seemed kind of smart, like his older cousin Rosie, who was always seeing right through him. *That's all I need right now!* On the other hand, he understood exactly how she felt. In fact, he felt that way most of the time at home, before everyone here thought he was someone important. Tommy melted.

"Horatio, Olly's right. We should let Raia come. I mean, it was really cool how she . . . saved him," Tommy said, glancing over at Olly. "I know I'm a wizard and all, but . . . well . . . Olly's never left Rolokon, and you've mentioned before that you've never traveled beyond Tacitonia, so it would be pretty helpful having someone who knows their way around."

Olly nodded vigorously, as did Raia.

Horatio looked from Raia to Olly to Tommy and threw up his hands. "Okay, okay. You all win."

"Thank you," Raia mouthed, and she smiled gratefully at Tommy.

"We've wasted enough time," said Horatio. "We must move on." And so they did, carefully skirting the treacherous mud.

LATER THAT DAY, THE SUN SANK IN THE SKY AND THE AIR cooled. Tommy groaned.

"Oh no."

"What?" Olly asked.

"I just felt a raindrop. If it's like last night, we can't stay outside. We'll be destroyed!"

"I don't think we'll be *destroyed*, Tommy," corrected Horatio, "but it *would* be best if we found somewhere to stay." He turned to Raia. "Now's your time to be helpful. Do you know of a place around here where we might take shelter?"

Raia nodded and pointed further down the road and off to the left. She pulled her mulion up front to take the lead and picked up the pace. After another few minutes of walking, she waved them to stop, handed Tommy the reins of her mulion, and disappeared into some bushes. When she reappeared, she motioned for them to follow.

By this time, heavy rain was falling. When the other three caught up with Raia, she was standing underneath a large slab of stone precariously supported on opposite sides by thick rocks—like a roof over two stubby walls.

"This is fine for us, Raia," said Horatio, "but what about the mulions?"

Raia pointed to a small, rocky hill a few yards away. Part of one side looked as if it had been gouged out by a bulldozer, leaving a shallow cave behind.

"Yes, yes, that should work." Horatio nodded, rubbing his hands to warm them. "We can put them in that hole. It should be pretty dry there. Very good indeed!"

The mulions fit nicely, and Olly removed their saddles and tied their leads to a nearby tree trunk. After feeding the animals and removing their own food and bedding, the travelers settled themselves at the center of their stone shelter, beyond the splashing rain. Then, after devouring meat sandwiches and fruit, they curled up under warm wool blankets and drifted off to sleep.

A few hours later, Tommy awoke to the sound of whinnying. *The mulions! They must be scared,* he thought. It was very dark, except for the flashes of lightning that brightened the sky. Everyone else was asleep. Tommy stood up, drawing his blanket tighter around him.

I should make sure they're okay. But just as he was about to dash out into the storm, he stopped. *Tirzah said there were devils and witches in the storm. Was she serious?* He sat back down. "There are no such things," Tommy told himself sternly. But just in case, he rummaged through his satchel and slipped his survival whistle and his pocket knife into his pants pocket before he ran out into the torrential rains.

Had he been able to hear the booming thunder and screams of wind, he might have hesitated a second time, for the storm was indeed terrible. He couldn't see a thing outside the shelter. A powerful gust of wind tore wet leaves from the tree branches and plastered them to his face and clothes. By the time he reached the mulions, he was soaked through. He entered the cave, wiping water from his eyes. The mulions were quite agitated, but he didn't see anything wrong. *It must just be the storm,* he thought. He spoke softly to them, gently patting each one, and refilled their water bucket from the small cask Olly had set outside to catch the rainwater.

As he was stroking Kia, lightning flashed and he thought he glimpsed a figure outside their shelter. *Who is out there?* He crept out of the cave, but as he stepped forward, *wham!* Something hard knocked him to the ground. Dazed, he lay still for a moment, his face pressed into the sloppy mud. Nothing felt broken, but when he tried to get up, he couldn't. Something heavy and rough was on his back. He turned his head sideways and was almost poked in the face by a tangle of tree twigs and leaves. *A tree fell on me,* he realized.

Tommy took a breath to call out for help, but his mouth snapped shut. *If I call them, Horatio and Olly will wonder why I couldn't use magic to escape. And Raia will definitely be on to me! I have to figure this out on my own.*

He wriggled around and discovered that he was caught in the tree's crown, away from the heaviest branches. His left arm was pinned to his side, but his right was free enough to get the knife out of his pocket. He slowly cut away at the twigs until his other arm was free and he could pull himself up through the remaining branches without shredding his skin. Just as he rose up, he saw Raia and Olly running out into the rain, with Horatio lagging behind.

"Tommy!" Olly exclaimed. "Are you okay? What happened?" Tommy turned to look at the tree, which was enormous. It had been uprooted by the fierce winds. *If I had been only a few feet nearer to the trunk . . .* He brushed the thought aside.

"Of course I'm okay, Olly!" Tommy said, trying to sound as indignant as possible. "It was nothing. A little spell to lift the tree and voila! I mean, if I couldn't get myself out of this, I wouldn't be a very good wizard, would I?"

"How stupendous!" Olly cried out, clapping his hands.

Out of the corner of his eye, Tommy saw Raia kneeling down where he had been trapped. She reached out a hand to touch the cut ends of the branches and looked over at him curiously. But then she just stood up and followed Olly, Horatio, and Tommy back to the shelter. As Tommy wiped off mud and peeled dead leaves from his skin, they stood, staring at him, with water dripping down their faces.

"Tommy," said Horatio, his hands on his chubby hips, "stupendous perhaps, but what were you doing? It's dangerous to be out during a storm. You should know that."

"It didn't *sound* dangerous. The only reason I was ever . . . uh . . ." Tommy stopped. He was about to say that the only time he was ever scared of storms was because of the thunder. But a real wizard wouldn't be scared of a storm. Plus, Raia was watching him intently, which made him uneasy. "Anyway . . . I . . . I knew I could handle it."

Horatio grunted and repeated his first question. "What were you doing?"

"Well, I heard the mulions. They were upset, and I wanted to check on them. Plus I had the itch."

"Itch?" asked Horatio, raising his eyebrows.

"You know. The itch! Well, that's what my . . . uh . . . head witch calls it . . . kind of. When I was a . . . uh . . . young . . . younger . . . wizard, she called it the Tuddleby trait."

"And what is that exactly?"

"It just means . . . I get an idea in my head, and I don't know, I can't just sit there. I need to do something about it. It's like . . . I get an itch and I have to scratch," Tommy said with a grin.

"Well, you scratched but good this time," said Olly, pointing to the scratches on Tommy's face and arms. They all laughed except Raia, who at least smiled. *Maybe she's not suspicious of me after all,* Tommy thought. He took a deep breath.

"Anyway, I thought I saw one of you leave the shelter so I stepped out of the cave, and that's when the tree came crashing down."

"I didn't leave the shelter," said Horatio. "Did either of you?" He turned to Olly and Raia, both of whom shook their heads.

"Oh," said Tommy. "I must have been mistaken." He bit his lip. He was *sure* he had seen a person outside the shelter. *Wait! What if it was the pearl thief?*

Horatio knelt down and straightened his blankets. "Enough excitement for one night, I would say. We have only a few hours until dawn. Let's get some sleep."

"Sleep?" cried Olly. "I couldn't possibly sleep now!"

Tommy and Raia nodded.

"Well, what do you suggest, Olly? A bedtime story?" Horatio chuckled.

"Actually, yes!" Olly exclaimed cheerfully. "That's a wonderful idea! What about a story from the *Book of Eldred*?"

"*Book of Eldred*?" asked Tommy. "That sounds really familiar."

"It's the middle of the night, Olly. Really!" griped Horatio.

Tommy turned and asked, "Horatio, did you tell me a story from there? Maybe the one you and Olly were telling me about—"

"Wait, wait," interrupted Olly. "Let me start—"

"I never said anyone should start!" protested Horatio.

Raia touched Horatio's arm. "Please, Sir Horatio," she mouthed.

"Yes, Sir Horatio," Olly implored. "I think we could all use something to distract us."

Horatio sighed and threw up his hands. "You win . . . again!" He turned to Olly. "All right, Olly, commence!"

Olly stood up, lifted his chin, and with a theatrical wave of his hand, began the tale.

"Ahem. Once upon a time, there was an enchanter who lived in a magical estate on top of one of the highest mountains. From there a grand river flowed through the four lands below, which together formed the kingdom of

Aesteron. It was the enchanter's responsibility to protect the kingdom from harm. The people who lived there knew nothing of him, and they were happy, and so he was content. But one day a terrible thing happened." Olly's face darkened, and he slowly scanned his audience as he whispered, "The enchanter's daughter was captured by an evil sorcerer!"

"Evil sorcerer?" said Tommy. "You mean the same one that stole color?"

"I guess. But that's not the point!"

"Horatio, is that the same sorcerer?"

Horatio yawned. "Possibly . . . It's been a while since—"

"Stop it!" Olly stamped his feet, exasperated. "That's not the point!"

"What is the point, Olly?" Horatio said tiredly.

"The point is . . . that just when all hope was lost, when the enchanter thought his daughter was gone forever, a dark and handsome stranger appeared and saved her!" Olly's voice rose with excitement. "And they fell in love! It's so beautiful," he sighed, his eyes growing misty. Tommy and Raia exchanged glances.

"What?" Olly said, annoyed, looking from one to the other. "What now? Why are you looking like that?"

"Sorry, sorry!" said Tommy, trying with some difficulty to keep from laughing. "It's just you're *so* dramatic."

"Enough!" said Horatio. "It's time for quiet and sleep."

"But Sir Horatio, there's so much more to tell!" objected Olly. "How the stranger left Rhian and then came back to be with her . . ."

Rhian. Just like Book of Eldred. Tommy bit his lip. *They both sound familiar. But where would I have heard them before?*

"Olly, enough storytelling. Another night perhaps."

"But—"

Horatio harrumphed. "Olly, Tommy, Raia, good night!"

The travelers settled themselves down as best they could. The ground was hard and pebbly, the storm still raged outside, and Tommy's mind raced as he tried to remember.

And then he did.

Tommy's eyes fluttered open. He knew exactly why those two names were familiar. He'd read about a place called Rhian in the book Uncle Thomas had left him. And the name of that book was *Book of Eldred.* He sat up suddenly. *How is that possible?*

"Horatio, are you still up?" whispered Tommy.

"Shhh," replied Horatio.

"Horatio, how'd you ever know about me in the first place? As a magician, I mean."

"You were written in the instructions. Go to sleep, Tommy."

"Instructions?" persisted Tommy.

Horatio looked over at him, annoyed. "The instructions! You're the only wizard mentioned."

"What do they say about me?"

"Honestly, Tommy, it's late and I'm very tired."

"I know. I'm sorry, Horatio. But it's important."

Horatio sighed. "Very well. The entry says something like, in case of emergency, contact Thomas something-or-other Tuddleby, wayfaring wizard of whimsy and so forth."

"It does?"

"Yes!" Horatio snapped. "But you probably forgot since the entry is from so long ago."

"How long?"

"I don't know. A hundred years maybe?"

"Th-that long, huh?" His eyes opened wide. Something was very wrong. Tommy had never even heard of this world! "Do you remember what the something-or-other between the Thomas and the Tuddleby was?"

"Why, your middle name, I would think. Din-something. Dinholm. Dinsmore . . . Dinsley. Yes, that's it, Dinsley!" Horatio yawned. "Tommy, I really must get more sleep. Good night, *again*." He flung a blanket over his head.

Tommy pulled himself up to lean against one of the shelter walls, staring at his muddy shoes. He was Tommy

Nathaniel Tuddleby. His uncle used to jokingly say he was "walking TNT," which he never understood until his dad explained that when he was a toddler he'd "explode" into a rage of tears for no apparent reason. His uncle . . . everyone called him Thomas, but Tommy vaguely remembered one time seeing him sign his name *D. Thomas Tuddleby* so maybe his *first* name was something like Dinsley? Anyway, Uncle Thomas was no wizard. He couldn't even do card tricks well!

I don't know what's going on, he thought, *but I'm not sure how long I can keep on pretending I'm a real wizard!*

Two nights ago, this had all been just a fun dream. It felt so great having everyone look up to him. But now he knew it was real. And it wasn't just that color was missing. Other things were going wrong. People couldn't talk. The weather was all messed up. And one thing he knew for sure. He didn't have any magical abilities. He badly wanted to tell Horatio and Olly the truth. *But if I say something, they'll think finding the pearls is hopeless. They'll give up. And everything will change.* And he didn't want that . . . at least, not yet.

Tommy glanced over at his companions. He thought he saw Raia staring at him, but when he looked again her eyes were closed.

For now, he would keep the truth to himself.

EARLY THE NEXT MORNING, THEY QUICKLY PACKED THEIR belongings and ate some biscuits and jam Temma had packed for them. While Tommy and Olly went to prepare the mulions, Horatio and Raia pored over a large map.

"How long will it take for us to reach the next land?" asked Tommy, mounting his mulion.

"That's just what Raia and I were working on," Horatio replied, rubbing his hands together and looking quite pleased. "Raia has been most helpful! It looks like we'll be able to save some time thanks to a shortcut she knows. We should be in Amorray by late afternoon. We may even be able catch up with the prince! Lead the way, Raia!"

Raia smiled at Horatio and nodded. She turned to Tommy, eyebrows raised, and mouthed slowly, "We need to talk." Tommy wasn't sure what she needed to talk about, but he suspected it wasn't anything good.

Magic Pebbles

The sun remained with them throughout the morning, and the travelers marveled at the sky's rich purple color. The fresh air smelled of wildflowers and pine trees. But except for the musical trilling of visiting birds and the clip-clop of the mulions' hooves on the dirt road, the land was silent.

By late afternoon, as Raia had predicted, they were nearing the border between Tacitonia and Amorray. The Collos River provided a natural boundary between the two lands; thus, they had to cross a bridge. That bridge, however, was a suspension bridge, old and rickety. Tommy stared in dismay at the sagging rope and plank structure, still soggy and slippery from the rains.

Raia, who was still leading the way, paused when they reached it. She dismounted her mulion and signaled for them all to do the same. She knelt down and pressed her fingers against the wooden planks, and then she motioned Olly over. He turned to Horatio and Tommy and said, "Raia thinks the wood is too soft and the bridge may not hold our weight. Maybe there's another way to cross, Sir Horatio?"

Horatio shook his head. "The next crossing is miles away, and Raia said that the terrain on this side of the river will grow more difficult to travel. It will add hours to our trip, and we haven't time. We must try to reach Amorray before the pearl thief does."

"Yes, but Sir Horatio, what if the bridge can't hold us? What if we fall? We could hurt ourselves." Olly was starting to panic. "And I can't swim. Isn't it better to find another way than *die*?"

"Olly, we're not going to die! We have a wizard!" Horatio put a hand on Tommy's shoulder. "Tommy will make sure we're safe. If he can lift a tree, he can certainly make sure the bridge doesn't fall apart on us! Right, Tommy?"

Tommy looked from Horatio to Olly, who was nodding vigorously, to Raia, who was eyeing him warily. Tommy coughed. His mouth opened as if to say something and then closed again. He nodded as he kept coughing. When his throat finally cleared, there was silence.

"Right," he said, realizing they were all expecting him to take charge. He thought for a moment and then cleared his throat again. "We'll go one at a time. I'll go first to make sure the bridge is safe. But first, I have something that will protect us." He rummaged through his satchel and pulled out four packages of Pop Rocks. "Hold out one of your hands, like this," he said, demonstrating with one hand out, palm up and slightly cupped. They did, and he ripped open the packages and poured one each into the palms of his companions and himself. Then he stuffed the empty packets back into his satchel before anyone could get a good look at them. "Now put these . . . uh . . . magic pebbles . . . in your mouth, but don't swallow. Let them just sit there. When they're done popping . . ."

"Popping?" Olly's eyes widened, and Horatio raised his eyebrows.

"Yes, popping. Once everything stops, the magical protection will be complete and we'll all be able to cross safely." And with that, he tipped the mound of Pop Rocks into his mouth. All the popping and fizzing in his mouth made him feel better somehow. Jake Jones was right: a little fun in a serious situation is not such a bad thing!

Raia grinned as the Pop Rocks crackled on her tongue. She nodded to Olly and Horatio, who exchanged glances and followed suit. When everyone confirmed that the "magic pebbles" were completely dissolved, they lined up behind Tommy.

The bridge creaked and swayed as Tommy crossed, but he reached the other end safely. He breathed in deeply. Now he just had to hope the others would be okay too.

He signaled for Raia to send the mulions across one by one. Then came Raia, and then Olly. With each crossing, the bridge swayed a bit wider and creaked a bit more. When at last it was Horatio's turn, he stepped gingerly onto the bridge, holding tightly to the ropes on either side.

He was almost across when the anchor at the far side loosened and the bridge dipped. Horatio lost his footing. He clutched the ropes on either side and caught himself from slipping backward.

Olly gasped. "Sir Horatio! Quickly!" Olly seized the bridge post in one hand and reached the other toward Horatio just as the bridge began to collapse. Olly stretched as far as he could and grabbed Horatio's wrist as he fell. Horatio shouted as his feet dangled over the river.

With Tommy's and Raia's assistance, Olly pulled Horatio to safety. Then they looked back up at where they had come. The bridge had disappeared, except for a few wooden slats dangling over the riverbed.

Horatio sat up slowly, massaging his wrist where Olly had grabbed him. He wiped droplets of sweat from his forehead and replaced his hat, which had fallen off as Olly yanked him from the bridge. "That was close indeed!"

Tommy extended a hand to Horatio and helped him to his feet. "I'm so sorry, Horatio . . . the . . . uh . . . spell wore off sooner than I expected . . ."

Horatio patted Tommy's arm. "No worries! If it hadn't been for that spell of yours, we wouldn't have been able to cross at all!"

Tommy smiled weakly. *A close call indeed.*

Only a few steps away from the bridge, a sign welcomed the travelers to Amorray. No sooner did they walk past the sign than they heard the rush of the Collos

River, the wind rustling leaves on a tree, and the loud crowing from a flock of birds overhead, silhouetted against a glowing orange sun.

"We can hear again!" exclaimed Tommy.

"With that ugly squawking, I would sooner have silence," grumbled Horatio.

"In my opinion, you have a very negative attitude, Horatio," said Tommy with a grin.

"I guess I do," admitted Horatio. "You're right. The squawking isn't so terrible. Sound *is* a wonderful thing. But what's happening to our kingdom is a terrible thing. What if we're too late to save Amorray's pearl? We still have several more hours to travel before we reach the city."

"Everything seems pretty normal so far," commented Tommy as he mounted his mulion, "except it's starting to get dark and I'm getting awfully hungry. Can we stop off somewhere—at least to eat?"

Horatio fished a map from one of the bags. He and Raia examined it, and when Raia pointed to a red dot on it, Horatio said, "Yes," nodding in agreement. "The town of Tingerton would be a good place to stop—it is just a few miles from here. And there's Amorray City, where we want to be," he added, pointing to a big black dot that lay an inch higher.

"Will we be sleeping there also?" asked Olly.

"No. There isn't much time, Olly, and we certainly can't waste any. I just want to be sure the pearl is safe."

As they followed the river upstream, the rich soil and ruby-red fields gave way to barren, rocky stretches of land. When they reached Tingerton, they found an inn, several stores, many small houses, and one enormous building with the words *TINGERTON FOUNDRY* carved over its main entrance.

"What's a foundry?" asked Tommy.

"It's a place where people work with metal," answered Horatio. "Just as Tacitonia provides grain to Aesteron, Amorray designs much of the metalwork. There are dozens of these foundries all over the land. But now," he said, jumping off his mulion, "I suggest we find ourselves something to eat."

The others dismounted as well, and they led the animals toward the inn and tied them to a pole at the front entrance. They then stepped into the large dining hall attached to the inn. Inside were benches and long tables, but few people.

A short girl who looked to be a few years younger than Tommy approached them, carrying a tray of food. She wore a white blouse and a blue skirt covered by a soiled white apron. "We're about to close, sirs . . . and ma'am," she added, nodding at Raia.

"Can't we be your last customers?" pleaded Tommy. "We're starving." He glanced over at his companions. "At least I am."

She dropped the food off with another customer and then disappeared behind a swinging door. Moments later, she poked her head out. "Pa says it depends on what you want to eat. He can't cook everything at all hours, you know."

"Anything will be fine," Horatio assured her. "We know it's late."

Once more the girl disappeared. They heard her shoes pattering against the wooden floor. When she returned, she was carrying four glasses of water. "Seat yourselves wherever you like," she said, but without giving the travelers a chance to decide, she set down the glasses at the nearest table. "How about here?"

They sat down. The girl stood before them, shifting her weight from foot to foot. "Where are you from? Are you foundry workers?"

Tommy shook his head and took a long drink of water. "No, we're here to catch the pearl thief," he said, wiping his mouth.

"You're crazy." She giggled. "I've never heard of any pearl thieves before."

Horatio glared at Tommy. "We're just travelers," he told her. "Nothing more."

"But he said—"

"I was joking," Tommy said quickly.

The little girl pursed her lips, swung around, and returned to the kitchen. When she returned, serving tray in hand, she gave each of them a large bowl containing spongy brown lumps mixed with bright orange, yellow, and red cubes. She placed a loaf of bread at the center of the table. Tommy looked at the bowl and made a face.

"What's the matter?" demanded the girl. "My pa makes the best organox balls in the world."

"It looks delicious!" exclaimed Olly. "I haven't had organox balls in a long time." He took a taste and nodded. "She's right. It's very good."

Tommy looked skeptically at them and then dipped his spoon into the bowl. Eyes closed tight, he shoved a spoonful of the stew into his mouth and chewed. His eyelids fluttered open. "Hey, it *is* good."

"Told you so!" The girl grinned. "So, what're your names?"

Horatio introduced them. "And yours?"

"Kayla."

"Tell me, Kayla, have you noticed anything odd lately? In the land, I mean."

She shook her head. "Why? Is there something going on?"

"Nothing at all," Horatio assured her.

Kayla sat with them while they finished eating, eyeing each of the newcomers and twirling her hair.

"How come she never says anything?" she asked, pointing to Raia. "Doesn't she know how to talk?" Raia glared at Kayla, slipped out from her seat, and stomped over to the other side of the room.

"Raia lost her voice when the pearl of Tacitonia went missing," replied Olly, glancing over at Raia.

"What do you keep talking about pearls for?" Kayla asked.

"Something's wrong with Raia," Olly whispered. "She's looked unhappy ever since we left the bridge. Did one of you say something to upset her?" Horatio and Tommy shook their heads.

"Do you have a place to stay tonight?" asked Kayla.

"We weren't planning to—" began Horatio.

"Can't we sleep for a few hours?" broke in Olly. "I'm exhausted."

"But . . ." Horatio looked over at Tommy, who was yawning every few minutes. "Well, all right then. For only a few hours. Could we stay next door?" Horatio asked the girl.

"You'll have to ask Pa about rooms."

"He owns the inn?"

"Uh-huh."

Kayla cleared away the dishes and Horatio followed her into the kitchen to speak with her pa. When they reappeared, Kayla led them through a doorway and up some stairs. She showed Raia to the first room off the stairway. Raia darted in and closed the door. Horatio, Olly, and Tommy would be sharing a room further down the hallway. Once there, she stayed for a few moments, silently watching them unpack their bags, and then giggled and left.

Tommy rolled his eyes as she closed the door behind her. "She's so annoying!"

"She's just a little girl, Tommy!" Horatio chided. "So, her father has promised to wake us up at dawn. That way we can reach the city early enough to make sure the pearl is safe."

"Raia looked so sad while we were eating. Maybe one of us should talk to her," suggested Olly.

Horatio nodded. "Why don't you go to her, Tommy? It must be very hard. Olly and I have lost our color, but losing your ability to speak is a much bigger problem."

Tommy sighed. He'd been avoiding one-on-one encounters with Raia ever since she gave him the "we need to talk" warning. "I'm not sure that's such a good idea, Horatio. I mean, being a wizard and all, I might be too intimidating."

Olly laughed. "Intimidating?"

Tommy scowled. "Yes, intimidating. Do you want to test me, Olly?" Tommy reached for his satchel.

Olly stopped laughing and shook his head vigorously. "No, no. Of course not."

"I know you're really much older, Tommy," said Horatio, ignoring them, "but you look about her age, so she may be more comfortable talking to you than either Olly or me."

Tommy took in a deep breath. "All right, all right, all right. Maybe I'll see if the Pop Rocks will cheer her up."

"Pop Rocks?" asked Olly. "What are those?"

"Huh?" Tommy looked up, startled, and then realized he'd forgotten where he was. "You know the . . . uh . . . magic pebbles we used to cross the bridge. Just a . . . uh . . . slang among us wizards!"

"But I thought those were to help keep us safe. Why would Raia need that?"

Tommy thought quickly. "They have many different uses. They can make people feel less sad because they're . . . uh . . . so . . . kind of . . . fun, right?"

"I guess so," said Olly slowly. "I just didn't know you could use magic things like that just for fun."

"Well, sometimes you can," said Tommy. "Anyway, it's getting late, like Horatio said. Have to go!" Tommy grabbed his satchel and hurried out.

Tommy Makes a Pact

Tommy knocked on Raia's door several times, to no response. He hoped there weren't any other guests, because he was making quite a racket. When she finally opened the door, she stood there with her hand on her hip and mouthed, "What?"

Tommy didn't have to hear her voice to know she was not happy to see him there. Her eyes were red, and her skin was blotchy.

"Can I come in?"

Reluctantly, she let him into her room and closed the door behind her. She stood silently, waiting for him to start.

"Listen . . . uh . . . are you all right? You seem really upset. We know it must be tough losing your voice and all . . . is that what's going on?"

Raia looked down at the ground. A few moments passed, and Tommy didn't know what else to do, so he continued, "I mean . . . like . . . it must be really hard to not be able to say anything. I get it."

"Really?" Raia mouthed and shook her head.

"Well, yeah, you're not the only one with troubles, you know!"

Raia kept shaking her head, hands still on her hips. Tommy was getting angry. "You think it's so easy being a wizard and all?"

Raia raised an eyebrow at him, then pranced in circles around the room and pretended to wave a wand back and forth.

"Hey, stop it! That's not fair! It's not what you think! I didn't ask to be here!"

Raia stopped abruptly and looked at Tommy, who realized he'd said more than he intended. She raised her eyebrows again.

Tommy scowled at her. For someone who had no voice, she had a lot to say. But there was something else. Tommy was feeling overwhelmed. He was beginning to make mistakes, and he desperately wanted to tell *some*one what was going on. She reminded him so much of Rosie, who drove him nuts . . . but Rosie never broke a promise.

"I have something . . . something . . . to tell you," Tommy began. "But I need to know I can trust you. Can I?"

Raia nodded her head vigorously.

"Hold on. Hold on!" said Tommy. "Look me straight in the eye and tell me you won't tell anyone anything I tell you."

Raia looked straight at Tommy—her eyes almost boring holes right through his head—and mouthed, "I promise."

Tommy looked back her, squinting hard. Jake Jones always said you can tell by a person's eyes if they're lying. Tommy wasn't actually sure what he should be looking for, but she seemed like she meant it.

Raia poked a finger at his chest. "You too," she mouthed.

"Yeah, sure. Of course!" Tommy promised. But none of this seemed like enough. "Hey, do you have a piece of paper and a pen?"

Raia shook her head.

"Hmm." Tommy looked around. "Actually . . ." He searched through his satchel. "I have something." He pulled out the thick pad of paper and a pen with the words *Spy Right* written across it. He wrote on the pad and then pushed the paper toward Raia.

Raia looked at Tommy, confused. There was nothing there. "Here," Tommy said, taking out the UV blacklight key chain. "Turn this on here." He pressed the button on the keychain. When he did so, dark blue words appeared on the paper.

Raia looked at Tommy with amazement.

"Just read what it says," said Tommy impatiently. "And sign."

On the paper Tommy had written, "Tommy and Raia do solemnly swear to tell the truth to each other always and never break a promise." Tommy had signed his name, and he pointed to where Raia should do the same. She nodded and signed. Tommy lit the keychain to reveal both of their signatures.

"And now, we'll have some Pop Rocks to kind of . . . cement things," he said. He removed a packet from his satchel. She looked at him, puzzled, and pointed to the packet. "I know, I know. Yes, we can use them. I'll explain later," he said as he emptied half the candy into her hand. "One . . . two . . . three . . . GO!" Together they poured the Pop Rocks into their mouths. They grinned at each other as the candy popped and fizzed in their mouths.

When all the Pop Rocks had dissolved, Tommy said, very seriously, "I have some stuff to tell you. Wait 'til I'm done before you say anything." And he told her his story, from the beginning. The true story.

When he was finished, he looked worriedly at Raia. "Are you mad? Do you think everyone will be mad?"

Raia shook her head and gestured for a piece of paper and the pen. "Thought *I* had problems!" she wrote. She grinned and then continued, "Figured something up. Knew you didn't lift tree. What now? Who thief?"

Tommy heaved a sigh. "I'm not sure."

"Olly?" Raia wrote down. "Could be pretending."

"No way! Olly wouldn't do that."

"People not always what they seem."

"There *is* someone I've been wondering about."

Raia looked at him questioningly.

"That prince. I mean, isn't it weird that he got back just when the pearl in Rolokon was stolen? And then he goes to Tacitonia and that pearl is stolen also?"

Raia shrugged.

Tommy peeked out her window curtain. "It's going to be light soon. I better get back." He peeled a few sheets off the pad and gave Raia the invisible-ink pen. "You take this in case we need to communicate with each other."

He walked toward the door, but Raia signaled for him to wait. She scribbled on the top sheet, ripped it off, and handed it to Tommy. She then opened the door and pushed him out, closing the door behind her.

Tommy stood outside the door. He flicked on the keychain so he could see what she'd written.

"We'll solve this. So you can <u>hear</u> me yelling at you!!!" He smiled. Raia wasn't so bad after all.

When Tommy returned to his room, the only sound was Horatio's spluttery snoring. He lay down on his cot and stared up at the ceiling. He was no closer to solving anything, but Tommy felt almost giddy. With Raia's help, they might just figure this out. And it felt so good to not have to always pretend he was someone he wasn't.

THE NEXT MORNING, A LOUD KNOCK ON THE DOOR
startled them awake. Kayla bounced into the room. "Wake
up!" she announced.

"We heard you," grumbled Tommy.

"Don't be such a grouch," chided the little girl. She
looked over at Horatio. "Why, Mr. Hue, you hardly have
any hair. Is that why you wear that big hat?"

Horatio blushed. "Of course not," he said, hastily
replacing the top hat on his bald head.

"Remember asking me if I noticed anything wrong
in the land?" she said.

"Yes."

"Well, now I do."

"What is it, Kayla?" Horatio asked, still sounding tired.

"Look for yourself." She walked over to the window
and drew open the curtain. All they could see outside was a
smoky mist. "It's also awfully warm outside. It smells funny.
And there are all these holes in the ground with steam
coming out."

"When did this begin?" asked Horatio.

Kayla shrugged. "This morning, I guess—although
Pa was telling me last night that it was getting pretty warm
out, at least warmer than usual."

"Is anything else wrong?"

"I don't think so. There was a fire in the foundry,
but nothing more than that. Breakfast is ready for you in

91

the dining hall, so don't be too long." And she skipped away.

"Maybe it's just a bad day out," suggested Tommy.

"I'd like to think so." Horatio sighed, unconvinced. "But thinking isn't good enough."

ONCE THEY HAD EATEN THEIR BREAKFAST AND THANKED Kayla and her father, the travelers hit the road. Amorray City was fairly close, but a thick, heavy smog blinded them and stung their eyes and the air grew increasingly rancid. And although the mulions had been fed and watered, they whined and shuffled their feet, struggling to turn back to Tacitonia.

Suddenly, a cracking sound echoed around them and Olly's mount brayed and danced sideways, nearly unseating the gangly man. Before Olly could do more than gasp, the roadbed cracked open, releasing a burst of steam. The other mulions shied around it.

Raia dismounted and stepped up to the crack.

"Don't do anything foolish, Raia," cautioned Horatio. "If it releases more steam, you may get burned."

Ignoring his warning, she knelt down and peered more closely into the crack and then jumped back with a nauseated look. She returned to the others, holding her nose and pointing to the crack.

"So that's where the smell is coming from. Something is definitely wrong," Horatio said. "We must keep moving!"

After another couple of crackles and near misses, Tommy said, "I have an idea. The mulions seem to know where the cracks are going to open." He jumped down and looked Kia in the eye, scratching behind her ear. "Kia," he said, "I know you want to go home, but we need to get to Amorray City. It's the only way to stop all this. Can you help us get there?"

The mulion stomped and huffed a bit but then looked him in the eye and took two steps toward Amorray City.

"Thank you." He remounted the mulion, gave her one more scratch and looked to the others. "Kia and I will lead. Just let go of the reins. The mulions will get us there safely."

The group proceeded carefully. The cracking sounds were enough to warn the mulions to avoid the fissures.

The four stayed close to the river—or at least what they hoped was the river—and as they went, the foul odor enveloped them. The temperature continued to rise. Kia stumbled on the rocky surface of the road, and Tommy saw that sweaty lather now blanketed her hide. "Maybe we should walk for a while and give the mulions a rest," he recommended. Raia nodded.

Olly jumped down from his animal and howled. "No wonder they're so jittery," he cried. "The ground is hot!"

"The pearl." Horatio frowned. "This all has to do with the pearl."

Tommy desperately wanted to lift his friend's low spirits, tell him that the pearl was safe, that they weren't too late. But he knew such words would be a lie, for something was indeed wrong.

After an hour of dreary travel, Raia tapped Tommy on the shoulder and pointed into the distance. Tommy peered into the smog. "Hey, look over there! There are people by the river!"

Olly and Horatio strained their eyes but could barely make out the several shadowy figures Tommy and Raia were pointing to.

"They're probably cooling themselves," said Olly, mopping his face with a cloth, "which seems a very wise thing to do. This heat is even worse than in Rolokon!"

No one greeted the adventurers as they approached. Some of the people were quenching their thirst with cupped hands, but most were filling buckets with water. Tommy tapped a small boy who was holding two pitchers on his shoulders.

"Excuse me, but what's going on here?"

The boy turned around. He wore only shorts. His face was flushed from the heat. "How should I know? Everything was fine yesterday."

"So everything just changed overnight?"

"I guess so. It seemed to start really late, though. There was a fire in the city's main foundry, so they had to close it down. And when I woke up this morning, my ma told me I had to go to the river because none of the water in the city was any good. How come *I* always have to do the chores?" he complained.

"My friends and I have come to help you." Tommy pointed to Raia, Horatio, and Olly. "We must make sure your pearl is safe."

"What's the matter with the pearl?"

"Nothing, we hope," said Horatio. "Do you know who the pearl guard is?"

"Of course! He's my uncle!"

"Well, he's the one we must speak to first. Could you take us to him?"

"Depends."

"On what?" Tommy demanded, but when he noticed the boy gazing wistfully at the mulions, he changed his tactic. "If you want, you can ride on my mulion."

The boy hesitated for a moment, studying them, and then nodded. Olly hoisted the boy into the saddle.

Tommy lifted the reins over the mulion's head. "My name is Tommy," he said, "and this is Kia. My friends are Olly, Raia, and Sir Horatio. What's your name?"

"Jem," the boy responded, holding the water pitchers tightly.

Jem led them into the center of the city, where the houses were clustered close together. It was very early in the morning, and on a typical day, the streets would have been empty. Now hundreds of people were milling about, trying to find out what had happened to change their formerly clean land into a dusty and smoggy one where huge black clouds hovered overhead.

As they walked, Tommy stopped abruptly. An odor, sweet and strong, punctured the stale city air. It reminded him of something familiar—like his grandfather's pipe tobacco. *No one should smoke on a dry day like this,* Tommy thought. He looked around. But with so many people, he couldn't find the culprit, and the aroma soon dissipated.

He started as a hand grabbed his wrist. He turned, and there was Raia, wagging a finger at him and yelling—well, he assumed that's what she was doing and was glad he couldn't hear. She looked at him questioningly, and he told her about the odor. She didn't seem concerned and motioned down a side street.

"We need to go," she mouthed. Tommy nodded.

A short distance away, they found the mulions hitched to a tree in front of a small wooden house. Jem led Tommy and Raia into a sitting room and introduced them to his uncle, Bram, before leaving to collect more water. Bram was a burly man dressed in overalls covered in ash and dirt. He remained standing, even though everyone else took a seat.

"Is the pearl okay?" Tommy burst out.

The man shook his head. "It's gone. Gone." His voice was weary.

"When did you first find it missing?" Horatio asked.

"Last night, before I locked up the foundry. I had been working late and nearly forgot to add the water to the pearl. When I went to do so—" He broke off, burying his head in his calloused hands.

"Have you any idea where it could be?" Tommy asked.

Bram shook his head. "I keep the pearl locked in a safe." He looked at Horatio ruefully. "Nothing like this has ever happened. Truly. I've never been so careless."

"I'm sure you weren't anything of the sort," Olly said sternly. "I guard the pearl in Rolokon, and it was also stolen. The same thing happened in Tacitonia."

"Stolen?!" Bram jerked his head up in astonishment.

"What did you think happened?" asked Tommy.

"I just assumed *I* had lost it. Who would want to steal our pearl?" Bram shook his head, puzzled. He stood up and walked over to the window, where he trailed his index finger across the glass, collecting a smudge of dirt. Then he gazed out at the misty land through the thin clear line his finger had left. He swung around. "Who would do such a thing?"

"I wish we knew," sighed Horatio. He turned to his companions. "It doesn't seem like Alexander has come through the city yet. Where could he have gone to?"

"Who?" asked Bram.

"Alexander, the prince of Aesteron. He left the palace days ago in search of the stolen pearls. We haven't seen him since. You haven't been questioned by any such person, have you?" the little man asked, a glint of hope in his eyes.

Bram shook his head.

"Horatio," interjected Tommy, "I've actually been meaning to ask you about that. I'm wondering . . . how well do you know the . . . uh . . . the prince?"

"What do you mean?"

"Well, he keeps not being places. What if . . ." Tommy paused and blushed as all eyes settled on him. "What if he's the thief?" he blurted out.

Horatio laughed. "Is that what's been worrying you?"

Raia rose to stand beside Tommy and nodded.

"Listen, both of you. I've known the prince since he was a child. He was always a good son and a loving brother. He has made many sacrifices for our kingdom. I'm not sure of the explanation, but I am certain there is one. Don't forget that he was with Violet at the palace when the pearl from Tacitonia disappeared. It couldn't be him!"

"I forgot about that," Tommy said ruefully. He sighed, muttering under his breath, "I should have thought of that."

Raia turned to face him. With hands on hips, she shot him a disapproving look.

"Don't give me that look!" he protested. "I said I forgot, okay?"

There was a loud bang on the door. Bram opened it and rushed back seconds later. "Hurry! We have to get more water. There's a fire blowing in toward the city center!"

The Mystery Deepens

Bram led the travelers to the river, carrying as many buckets as they could find. Just a few hundred feet away, orange and red flames shot into the sky. They hadn't gone far when Horatio stopped. "The prince! He's over there," he cried out excitedly. "Prince Alexander!" he shouted, waving.

Tommy saw a man sitting on an animal that resembled a horse, except it was striped like a zebra. The man turned his head. Horatio ran the short distance to him and spoke a few words. The man grasped Horatio's hand and then dismounted. He was quite tall.

Horatio brought him over to the group and pronounced, "My friends, it is my greatest honor to introduce His Highness, Prince Alexander."

As Horatio introduced each of the travelers in turn, Tommy gazed up at the handsome face of the prince, who stood confidently before them, alert and strong. His blue eyes twinkled, and his hair flowed in thick dark ripples.

When Tommy's turn came, Alexander shook his hand. "So you are the famous magician who has come to help us?"

Tommy nodded. "Yes, sir."

The prince studied him. "You are somewhat young, are you not? To be such a powerful magician, I mean."

Tommy swallowed. "Age isn't exactly everything, sir. Plus I'm *a lot* older than I look."

"He's quite good, Prince Alexander!" piped in Olly. "Sir Horatio and I have seen him do many wonderful things. Why, he saved Sir Horatio from the spiderweb and used magic pebbles to help us cross the bridge safely, and he lifted a huge tree all by himself!"

Tommy blushed. He looked over at Raia, who was working hard to keep a straight face, and reddened even more.

"Enough, Olly," interrupted Horatio. He turned to the prince. "Did you just arrive?"

"Yes, this very moment." Alexander gazed around him, shaking his head. "But I can see I was too late."

"You know the pearl in Tacitonia was never found."

"I know I could not find it."

"But where have you been all this time? No one saw—"

"We really must go, Sir Horatio," Bram interrupted. "The fire."

"Yes, of course," said Horatio, flustered. He looked up at Alexander. "Where can we meet you? We must talk."

"Hurry!" Bram repeated urgently. He nodded toward Alexander. "Perhaps you, too, could help us."

"Of course. We will need everyone's help to bring this under control," Alexander said grimly.

"But you're a prince," cried out Horatio, appalled. "We need to protect you!"

"Sir Horatio." Alexander looked down at the little man with a kindly expression. "I know you are worried, but I must help. I could not live with myself if I stood by and did nothing."

"Look!" Bram pointed. The fire had grown fiercer and was creeping closer. Clouds of black smoke billowed in the air. It would be disastrous for the fire to reach the city center. It was already too near.

THEY JOINED HORDES OF PEOPLE COLLECTING RIVER water in pitchers, cups, and washbasins—anything they had. Everywhere people were coughing. Tommy heard anxious voices coming toward them from the direction of the fire, shouting "Hurry! Hurry!" He looked up as a man laid a young boy on the ground.

Tommy recognized him—Jem!

Jem's eyes were closed, his body limp, but Tommy could see his chest slowly rising and falling. He was alive! Bram and Alexander dropped their buckets and rushed toward him, pushing everyone out of the way. "Let me through!" Bram yelled. He knelt beside Jem, who had begun coughing.

Moving quickly, Alexander scooped Jem up in his arms. "I'll look after him."

"But Your Highness, I can't—"

"Please." Alexander touched Bram's arm. "Please. He just needs some fresh air and clean water to drink. You are needed here. I will take good care of him. I promise."

"Thank you," Bram said gratefully.

With that, Alexander sprinted downstream, carrying Jem away from the smoke and fire while Bram ran toward it.

Tommy began to follow Alexander, but Raia blocked his way. She pointed to the fire. Tommy understood. He was supposed to be the wizard. They would expect him to help with the fire. "Let's go!" she mouthed.

Reluctantly, Tommy picked up the heavy buckets and ran as quickly as he could, following Raia. From what anyone could tell, the fire had started at the outskirts of a neighboring village where there were few houses but many sun-scorched trees and fields. No one knew what or who had caused it, but because of the dry weather, the flames grew and spread rapidly. Men and women ran as near as they dared to the burning orange blazes, emptied their containers of water, and then backed away, gasping for air, the fumes burning their throats.

Bram ordered the villagers to form a chain from the river so they could move water more quickly. At first it seemed they were making some progress, but then a ferocious gust of wind whipped the fire around them. Everyone watched in terror as the flames encircled them. It seemed that nothing could stop the blazing monster—and now they were trapped.

"Can't you do anything?" Horatio cried out to Tommy over the sound of crackling flares and panicked villagers. Tears streamed down his cheeks in the gritty smoke.

Raia looked worriedly at Tommy. Tommy looked back helplessly. He closed his stinging eyes and covered them with his hands, as if by not looking he could make everything go away.

And then it did.

The flames died down as if someone had blown out a flickering birthday candle. People looked up in amazement as the hot crimson wall collapsed into orange embers. Everyone rushed to douse the last remnants of the fire.

The impossible had happened. The fire had been extinguished. People cheered, still covered with dirt and soot. Some had been injured. Most were coughing and sputtering, but the air miraculously cleared of smoke.

Tommy whispered to Raia, "What just happened?" Raia slowly shook her head.

Horatio walked over to Tommy. "Was it you?" he asked quietly. "Was it your magic that ended the fire?"

Tommy was dumbfounded. What could he say? He wasn't a magician, but no one other than Raia could know—at least not yet, not until they could make sense of things. What bothered him most was that Horatio was right. Only magic could have ended the fire. So if *he* didn't have the magic, who did?

Raia clapped her hands, pointed to Tommy, and copied what he had done just before the fire was extinguished, dramatically covering her eyes and looking as if she were muttering an incantation under her breath. Horatio nodded.

Just then, Alexander ran up from behind them. "Sir Horatio . . . what . . . ?"

"Jem!" exclaimed Bram. "Is Jem okay?"

"Yes," Alexander assured him. "He will be fine. He's resting but . . . but what happened here?" Alexander turned to Horatio and Tommy. "I heard screams and was coming back to help, and then . . . the fire, it just disappeared! I've never seen anything like it!"

Horatio nodded toward Tommy.

Alexander smiled and said quietly, "Of course. It could only have been magic."

"Thank you, Mr. Tuddleby." Bram bowed his head. "We are indebted to you. You saved us all."

Tommy squirmed. He glanced at Raia, who almost imperceptibly nodded. Tommy took a deep breath and looked up at Bram. "You are . . . you are most welcome."

Horatio patted Tommy's back, beaming proudly. "Indeed!"

ONCE THEY WERE CERTAIN OF THEIR SAFETY, THE TRAVELERS returned to Bram's house, where Alexander told them of his adventures.

"I reached Tacitonia and was heading to meet the pearl guard when I heard that the innkeeper had rented a room to a stranger. The stranger had arrived in Tacitonia the day before the pearl was found missing and had checked out of the room only a few hours earlier."

"That must be the pearl thief," Horatio said grimly.

Alexander nodded. "I had heard that the pearl was simply misplaced, but it seemed far too coincidental that the pearl would disappear while this mysterious person was in Klaton. So I decided to pursue them and see what I could find out."

"Prince Alexander, you should not have taken such a risk!" objected Horatio. "You are too important. What if you had been hurt?"

"Not to worry, Sir Horatio," Alexander said ruefully. "Unfortunately, I had no luck in finding anyone of the sort and only succeeded in wasting valuable time. I decided to continue on to Amorray rather than double back to Klaton in the hopes that I could warn you in time, Bram."

"But you were at least a day ahead of us, and the pearl went missing only last night," said Tommy. "What happened?"

Before Alexander had time to respond, Olly cleared his throat. "Er, remember, the bridge from Tacitonia was . . . not safe. If it weren't for Tommy, why, we would never have been able to cross!"

"Yes, Olly." Alexander nodded. "That is where things went wrong for me as well, so—"

"So you must have gone to the other crossing." Horatio shook his head. "Oh, Prince Alexander, that crossing was miles away. No wonder you didn't get here in time!"

"Plus you didn't have Raia to help you," added Olly. "Raia knows her way around the kingdom better than anyone, and she has already saved us so much time!"

Alexander looked over at Raia thoughtfully. "How wonderful to have someone like that with you." He turned back to Horatio. "Sir Horatio, I sent word of my whereabouts to Violet and left specific instructions that everyone was to stay at the palace. I need to make sure Violet is safe. No one means more to me." Alexander wagged a scolding finger at Horatio, but his tone was playful. "You should not have disobeyed me."

Horatio, missing the prince's joking tone, was distraught. "I am so very, very sorry, my dear prince," Horatio said, speaking more quickly as he continued, "I truly did not mean to. Truly! It's just . . . Queen Violet insisted. And . . . and . . . what choice did we have? And you need us here, Prince Alexander! Especially Tommy. Tommy might be the only one who can help us." Horatio's face was quite red now, and he swiped his handkerchief across his forehead.

Alexander, looking as if he was trying not to laugh, held out his hand, gesturing for Horatio to stop.

"Please do not upset yourself, Sir Horatio." The prince patted Horatio's arm kindly. "I know you meant well and want nothing more than to make sure our kingdom is secure. What you say makes good sense."

"Thank you, Your Highness, thank you indeed." Horatio settled back in his chair, heaving a sigh of relief.

Alexander stood up and paced back and forth. "We must form a plan." The others looked on as he stopped and scanned the room until his eyes settled on Tommy. "How are we to do it? How can we stop this pearl thief?"

"He's probably heading toward Tangoria," said Olly.

"*She* might be too," piped up Tommy.

"What she?" Horatio asked, a hint of irritation in his voice.

"The same she that's the he! Why can't he be she?"

"He's perfectly right," said Alexander. "We can't be sure *who* is doing this."

"So we should go to Tangoria, then," said Horatio.

"That would seem best. But I can travel much faster on my horse than you can on your mulions. Why don't we split up? I will go directly to Tangoria and meet with the pearl guard while you investigate the thief's trail. We can meet somewhere to share what we have learned."

"You're not coming with us?"

"It's getting late. It makes much more sense for me to push ahead."

"But—" Horatio began.

"We have no choice, Sir Horatio!" Alexander said sternly. "We have to protect our kingdom and catch this thief."

Horatio nodded, "Yes, of course. Whatever you think best."

Tommy and Raia exchanged looks. Horatio was clearly trying to avoid another scolding.

Alexander continued, "Once I find out about the pearl in Tangoria, I'll meet you at Pubstin, an island in the Lake Escape. We can rest there and plan our next move."

"But what if you run into trouble?" asked Horatio worriedly. "This pearl thief could be very dangerous!"

"I will be careful, Sir Horatio," Alexander assured him. "If you do not find me at Pubstin, continue on to Wentree Place. I will meet you there. And I promise not to take any action without first consulting you."

Horatio looked relieved. "Thank you, Your Highness. Queen Violet would never forgive me if anything happened to you."

Alexander bent down to collect his bag. "I must be off," he said, striding toward the door. He paused and turned to Tommy. "I've heard, Mr. Tuddleby, that Pubstin has a drink called the House Specialty that is supposed to be quite delicious. You all must try it. We can celebrate your success with the fire, and who knows? Maybe Tangoria's pearl will be safe and we'll have something more to celebrate." He smiled at the companions. "Wish me well."

"That would be something to celebrate indeed!" agreed Horatio, and they all nodded. "Be well, Prince Alexander. Be well." And with that, the prince disappeared into the still-misty air.

As they washed up and prepared to move on, Bram thanked Tommy again and again for saving Amorray from certain destruction. Tommy accepted his thanks graciously but said nothing else. The pieces of this puzzle were scattered all over, and he couldn't make any of them fit. Plus, something else was gnawing at him, though he couldn't put his finger on it. He caught Raia's eye and knew she was thinking the same thing.

The House Specialty

I t was growing dark when the travelers reached a three-way intersection marked by a large painted sign. Ahead was Tangoria. To the right, Pubstin. Behind them, Amorray was still covered in charred, smoldering clumps of ash and foul-smelling smog. Things were far from well.

"That's where we want to be," said Horatio. He checked his pocket watch. "We're making good time. We might even be able to eat before meeting Prince Alexander."

The farther they traveled from the main road, the more the smog thinned and the pungent odor subsided. The travelers inhaled huge gulps of fresh air and felt the sting leave their eyes.

"What land is Pubstin in?" asked Tommy.

"The Lake Escape," replied Horatio.

111

"What's that?"

"Pubstin is an island that lies at the tip of Lake Calimar. It is independent from all the lands, although it does belong to the kingdom."

After a couple more miles of travel, they heard sounds of music and, rounding one more bend, came to the edge of the lake. A short distance from shore, a large tavern, constructed of crystals and decorated by colorful lanterns, stood on the island.

"Come in! Come in!" a voice called to them from the island. "Just use the bridge."

When they stepped off the wooden bridge, the same voice announced, "Welcome to Pubstin, friends. Your faces are new to me. Have you never been here before?" And there, in front of the tavern door, stood a tall man with rosy cheeks and a potbelly, clasping his hands in delight.

Horatio cleared his throat. "Sir—"

"Please do not call me 'sir,' sir. My name is Myrick. I am your host tonight," the man gushed.

"Then Myrick," Horatio began again, "could you tell us if the prince, Alexander, has entered your establishment tonight?"

"Prince Alexander? Here? Why, I thought he was still cavorting about in distant lands," exclaimed Myrick.

Horatio cleared his throat. "Well, with King Tintoretto's—"

"Of course the prince would have to return for *that*," Myrick cut in. "The dear man was such a good king. But the prince? He's supposed to be here? We must have a celebration!"

"I don't think that's such a good idea, Myrick. The prince wouldn't want to cause any fuss. Anyway, we have little time to waste. We're on our way to Tangoria, and—"

Myrick crinkled his face in extreme distaste. "Tangoria? You certainly don't want to be there tonight, nor would you want to be in Amorray. It is here, here, here, where you want to be, be, be," he bellowed, sweeping his hand to and fro with each repetition. "And it would make me quite sad if you don't stay." He added a dramatic sniffle.

Raia tapped Tommy on the arm. "We *do* want to be in Pubstin," she mouthed, motioning toward Myrick. If she exaggerated every word and spoke slowly, Tommy could understand her pretty well.

"Yes, that's right," Tommy said. "In fact, we *have* to be in Pubstin, don't we?" He nodded to Horatio and Olly, who reluctantly nodded back. Myrick looked much relieved. "Are you sure the prince isn't here yet?"

"Certainly! I would know about such things," said Myrick, fluttering his eyelashes and sniffing deeply through his nose. "If you'd like, I *could* check the register. But let's not stand out here. We'll talk inside, where it's fun!" He giggled.

Myrick let out a whistle, and a young boy appeared, took the mulions' reins, and led the animals away. The travelers followed Myrick through a bright pink door.

They entered a large room furnished with small round tables and crowded with people laughing and talking. The sun's rays entered through the crystal walls as it set, shooting rays of color across the room. In the center of the room, a spiral staircase decorated with pink and purple ornaments led to a platform where a small band of musicians played. Some people were dancing. Others crowded around a counter, indulging in multicolored drinks.

"Wow!" squealed Tommy, his eyes lighting up with excitement. "This is going to be great!" Raia gazed around the room, wide-eyed, and nodded. They followed Myrick to one of the few unoccupied tables.

"Now!" Myrick clapped his hands. "Why doesn't the little boy come up with me. House Specialties all around!" He squatted down and tapped Tommy on the nose several times, tittering. "You'll *love* the House Specialty."

"House Specialty!" exclaimed Tommy. "That's what Prince Alexander told us we should get!"

"Right!" Myrick scooped Tommy up onto his back and hopped away.

When Myrick and Tommy returned, bearing four huge drinks, their host informed them, "The prince hasn't come yet." He placed a drink, each the size of a large ice cream sundae, in front of each of them. "Well, what are you waiting for?" He pushed one glass closer to Tommy and another closer to Raia.

They stared down at the concoctions. Pieces of fruit resembling cherries, oranges, lemons, limes, and blueberries floated on top of layers of red, orange, yellow, green, and blue liquid. When they lifted their glasses, the colors mixed together. Tommy was the first to take a sip. The liquid tasted as sweet as chocolate, but then salty like potato chips. As it rolled down his tongue, his lips puckered at a sour flavor, and the very last tasted like bitter lemon juice. Tommy scrunched up his face while the others watched in amazement.

"What a drink!" he exclaimed once his lips had unpuckered. "Every color is different. Try it!" Raia took a sip of hers as Tommy pushed two glasses toward Horatio and Olly. Raia's face broke into a wide grin—the biggest they'd seen since meeting her.

Horatio pushed the drink away. "No, Tommy. We must ask Myrick some questions." He turned to their host. "Have you heard of any problems in Tangoria?"

"Tangoria? No, I don't think so." Myrick jiggled his head. "Why should there be any problems? In fact, why in the world are we worrying about such ridiculous things as problems? We're in the Lake Escape. It's against the house rules."

"House rules, you say?" interrupted Olly, absentmindedly watching Tommy slurp his drink, pucker his lips, and exhale a breath of satisfaction. Slurp. Pucker. Exhale. Slurp. Pucker. Exhale.

"Yes," said Myrick. "They state that it's rude for you not to try the House Specialty at least once."

Olly looked up quickly. "Well, if it's against the rules, then maybe—"

"I don't think so, Olly," said Horatio.

"But what can it hurt?"

"If you don't drink anything now, soon there won't be any left!" chortled Myrick. He grinned at Tommy. "The little chap certainly likes those drinks, don't you, little chap?" He pinched one of Tommy's cheeks. *Stop treating me like a baby,* Tommy wanted to say, but his lips were too puckered to talk.

"It's our duty, Sir Horatio. The prince told us *we must,* and we can't deny Myrick's hospitality. After all, we represent the queen!" coaxed Olly. He tasted the odd liquid. "It *is* good."

Myrick hiccupped proudly. "Well, friends," he said, rising. "Is there anything more I can do for you?"

"No, Myrick," replied Horatio. "But please tell us when the prince arrives. It's most urgent!"

"Of course! Of course! Well I *really* must be going now. Ta-tee-ta, my dears. Enjoy yourselves. Everyone always does!" And, with a parting wave, Myrick disappeared through the crowd.

More people entered the tavern and pushed and jostled their way through the crowd. Everywhere, the travelers heard the tinkle of toasting glasses, laughter following a good joke, and cheers for a couple dancing wildly to the music.

Olly finished his drink, looked up, and stared at Tommy. "Your tongue, Tommy!" Then he turned to Raia. "And you too!" He started to laugh.

"What? What?" Tommy demanded. He stuck out his tongue and looked at it, cross-eyed. "I can't see anything. What are you laughing at?" He stuck out his tongue again, then turned to Raia. "You stick out your tongue so I can see!"

Raia, doubled over with laughter, shook her head.

"It's all different colors!" exclaimed Olly. Tommy rolled his eyes and looked over at Horatio. "Come on, tell me the truth."

"That *is* the truth, Tommy," Horatio said with a nod.

"Olly, let me see yours."

Olly shook his head. "Uh-uh."

"Raia, let me see!" Tommy said, exasperated. She stuck out her tongue. The drink had stained it with stripes of red, orange, yellow, green, and blue.

"Can we have one more drink?" pleaded Tommy.

Horatio examined his pocket watch. "Where could he be?"

"Who?"

"Alexander. He's who we're waiting for, remember?"

Tommy stilled. "Oh. I forgot."

"Me too," said Olly. "I'm still thirsty, Sir Horatio. Why *don't* we have another?"

Horatio sighed. "Why not, I guess." He picked up his drink. "We must wait for Alexander—and I am rather thirsty. Lead us on, Tommy. You know where to go."

Once they had collected their drinks, they tried to return to their original table but couldn't push their way back. Fortunately, another table opened up, and they claimed it. Tommy started to say something, but Raia clapped her hand over his mouth and motioned at the two women who had just sat down at the next table.

"Are you sure, Seraphina?" the smaller of the two women was asking, her lips pursed.

"I saw it bright as day, Ezmee. You think I should tell someone?" responded her friend, a hefty woman with curly orange hair and a loud, brassy voice.

"What *exactly* did you see?"

"Why, it was when I was coming up to Pubstin this afternoon," said Seraphina. "I was up at my inn in Amorray. I tell you, Ezmee, it's lucky I'm not in the city 'cause it's just horrid 'round those parts." She took a large forkful of food and stuffed it into her mouth. "Anyway," she continued after gulping it down, "it was by the intersection, to one side. No one was around, 'cept myself, and I stayed a distance away so he wouldn't see me."

Tommy looked at his companions. "Hey, you think they're talking about—"

This time Olly clapped a hand over Tommy's mouth. "Shh. Listen."

"The thing is—" Seraphina sat back in her chair and chewed. "The thing is," she repeated, "I thought he was just a regular traveler until he lifted his hand. You'll never guess what I saw, Ezmee. You'll *never* guess."

"Seraphina!" blazed her friend. "Just tell me."

"No need to get all upset!" chided Seraphina. She lowered her voice, and the travelers strained to hear her. "What I saw was him takin' somethin' from his pocket. And Ezmee, it was beautiful. Just beautiful. All these rays of light shootin' here and shootin' there." Seraphina waved her arms in every direction.

"You're puttin' me on."

"No, I'm not," the bigger woman insisted. "Anyway, it was gettin' late, so I started walkin' toward the intersection—but slowly, so I could still catch what was goin' on. Soon as he saw me bumblin' along, he started walkin'. Then I stopped, like I didn't know which road to take—just standin' there with my hand over my mouth, and my eyebrows all wrinkled up in confusion. He passed by me, headin' down the road to Frumbut."

119

"Well, did you see anything else?"

Seraphina shook her head. "No, but he sure smelled sweet."

"What *are* you talkin' about?"

"A nice, sweet odor . . . musky."

Ezmee rolled her eyes at her friend. "Seraphina, you're crazy. Who do you think it was?"

"Well, I've been hearin' about this pearl business. And they say there's a magician that's come from a long way away to help save everything. I make a bet it's him."

"I don't know," Ezmee said doubtfully. "It could just be the sun playin' tricks."

"Believe what you want, but I know what I saw. And anyway, I got *fee*lin's. Unexplainable *fee*lin's. Guess you could call it *in*tuition. But come on, Ezmee, I'm still hungry. Besides"—she glanced sideways at Horatio as she rose from her chair—"there isn't much privacy if you want to talk around here." And she brushed by Horatio's chair, followed by Ezmee, who looked sternly at Olly and tilted her chin up.

"I see what you mean, Seraphina. I see what you mean."

The two women bustled away, leaving the travelers to make sense of Seraphina's words.

"That was interesting, wouldn't you say?" Tommy said. "I wonder who the man was. What do you think, Olly?"

"Well, if you're the magician, then—"

"—then he must be the pearl thief," concluded Tommy.

"We can't be sure of that," Horatio said. "Ezmee's right. Maybe the flashing light was just the sun."

"Or maybe that was a signal, and he's having a secret rondayview with his helper," Tommy declared, folding his arms in front of his chest.

"That's *rendezvous*, Tommy, as well as nonsense. The drink must be affecting you," Horatio said testily. "But I do wonder who that man could have been."

"Well, I'm tired," Tommy said, and immediately yawned. "What time is it?"

"Is anyone hungry?" asked Olly. "Maybe we could get something to eat. I'm feeling a bit queasy. All the noise and the lights and the colors. It's quite overwhelming!"

Seeing Raia's and Tommy's answering nods, Horatio pushed his chair back from the table. "That seems like a very good idea."

Myrick swooped in, shouting, "Did I hear you say you're hungry? We have a wonderful buffet! The prince still hasn't arrived, by the way, but have another House Specialty!"

"Who?" asked Tommy.

Myrick looked at him and burst out laughing. "It works every time!"

"What works every time?"

"The House Specialty!"

"What do you mean?"

"I told you before, house rules!"

"What do you mean?" Tommy pressed, confused.

"I already *told* you. The Lake Escape is not for problems! And the House Specialty helps you forget about all those *boring* to-do lists so you can focus on being here, here, here!" Myrick twittered, gesturing all around.

"Huh?" Tommy turned to his friends. "What is he talking about?"

They all looked as confused as he felt. What were they supposed to do next, other than eat?

Horatio and Olly soon returned with four plates of food, which they all polished clean. No sooner had they finished than Raia folded her arms on the table, laid her head down, and fell fast asleep. It was quieter now, without so much confusion and commotion, and shortly her companions did the same.

When they awoke the next morning, the four travelers found they weren't alone. A chorus of a hundred snores filled the room. A sleeping customer sprawled across almost every table, and the hall was in a jumble, with tables and chairs tipped over and paper streamers strewn across the floor. Several people were quietly mopping the floor and righting the furniture.

Horatio sat up. "Where are we? What happened?" He checked his pocket watch. "Oh dear! It's already late in the morning. Weren't we supposed to meet Prince Alexander?"

Tommy stood. "Something's not right," he muttered. He spotted their host and waved him over. "Myrick, what happened to us? Did Prince Alexander show?"

"Prince Alexander? Was he supposed to come? I *completely* forgot! Oh my! We would have shown him such a marvelous time! So sad we missed him!"

"What if he came and couldn't find us?" Horatio said, quite upset. "You were supposed to let us know when he came. We have urgent business, Myrick! We couldn't afford to stay here all night!"

"I'm so sorry to hear that, my little man," said Myrick. "I would have certainly brought him to you if I had *seen* him. But alas, alas, alas I did not. Things are very lively at Pubstin, you know, and I become so *distracted*. As did *you,* it seems." He grinned at them and winked. "Frankly, my dear fellows, I never recommend the House Specialty if you can't afford to forget for just a little bit. That's the whole *point* of the House Specialty! It's what we're *famous* for! Toodle-do!" Myrick ran off to check on his other guests.

Horatio shook his head unhappily. "I *knew* we shouldn't have had those drinks. I have a terrible feeling the prince is in grave danger. We must leave quickly!"

"Why don't we ask that man for directions?" suggested Olly, pointing to one of the moppers. "I bet the locals know the fastest way to get there."

"Good thinking," replied Horatio. "In fact, come with me. I've noticed you have a very keen sense of direction." He led Olly, who looked quite pleased with himself, toward the man.

As soon as they left, Raia touched Tommy's sleeve and pulled him toward her. "Something's not right."

"Yeah, I know."

"He knew."

Tommy looked confused. "Who knew? Knew what?"

"He knew—" but then she stopped as Horatio headed back to their table. She put her finger to her lips.

Tommy nodded. "We'll talk later," he whispered.

"Apparently we don't have to go all the way back to the main road," said Horatio. "That should save us some time. Come along—Olly's getting directions to Wentree Place."

They joined Olly just as the man said, "Just follow the signs to the town center. Can't miss it."

They thanked him and collected the mulions. After crossing the bridge, they followed the sign toward Tangoria, leaving Pubstin far behind.

The Pearl Thief Revealed

As they crossed into Tangoria, keeping the Collos River within sight, Tommy watched for the destruction and danger that followed the stolen pearls. But the valley was lovely. The river flowed freely, and trees in the distant fields looked heavy with ripe fruits. Tingling fresh air accompanied the cloudless sky, and on either side of them lay glorious mountains.

"Why, this land is so beautiful!" exclaimed Olly. He jumped down from his mulion, ran to one of the many bushes bordering the road, and returned with a handful of succulent-looking orange berries. "These are perrirazimus berries," he announced with an air of dignity. "They are often used in pies and are quite delicious!"

"Can we eat them?" asked Tommy.

"Of course!"

Tommy playfully snatched one berry. But no sooner did he pop it in his mouth than the grin on his face vanished and the color drained from his cheeks. He spit out the berry, coughing and choking. Raia quickly handed him a water canteen.

"What happened?" both Horatio and Olly demanded as Tommy finished drinking.

"The berry," Tommy sputtered. "The skin was so salty, and when I bit into it, it burned."

"Burned?" Olly exclaimed in disbelief. "It couldn't burn. That's impossible."

"Couldn't you have been wrong? I wasn't acting, you know. It feels like I burned my whole mouth," said Tommy. And now his stomach was cramping too.

Olly shook his head, puzzled. Raia approached him and plucked one of the berries he held. She licked the outside, looked up at Olly, and nodded. Olly placed the berries on a nearby rock and took a cup and a knife from his knapsack. He filled the cup with water before he cut one of the berries in half—making sure to avoid the juice—and dropped it into the cup. Everyone watched in amazement as the water clouded and sizzled.

"No wonder," Olly muttered, shaking his head again.

Horatio gazed around them. "We're too late."

"What?" Olly said, puzzled.

"It has to be the pearl. We must hurry. Something is dreadfully wrong."

"Where should we go first?"

"We should meet Alexander. Then we'll find out about the pearl."

THE SUN WAS STARTING TO SET WHEN THEY FOUND Wentree Place. They had just sent the mulions to the stable with a worker when they bumped into Alexander, who was coming from the direction of the stable.

"You're safe!" exclaimed Horatio. "We were so worried."

"I'm sorry I couldn't meet you at Pubstin, but I thought I'd found our thief and never even made it to Tangoria." He shook his head ruefully. "Once again, I was wrong."

"Have you heard anything about the pearl here?"

"No. I still have to see the pearl guard. Why? Have you heard anything?"

"Something is very wrong," said Olly. "Tommy was poisoned by a perrirazimus berry. And that shouldn't be. They're used all the time."

"In the best of pies," added Tommy, clenching his hand to his stomach, which was still upset.

"You think the pearl's been stolen?" asked the prince.

All four travelers nodded at once. Horatio turned to his companions and said, "Wait here. I'll go with the prince and we'll find out what we can."

Alexander shook his head. "No, Sir Horatio. It's getting late. Please send word to Violet so she knows where we are and that we are tracking the thief. She must be terribly worried. I'll find the pearl guard and meet you back here."

"Of course!" Horatio bowed.

Alexander mounted his horse and headed toward the town center. Horatio requested rooms from the innkeeper and then told Olly, "I need to go to the town office to send the message to Queen Violet. And then I'll see what I can find out from the villagers. Maybe someone saw something." He motioned to Tommy. "Why don't you see if you can do something for Tommy? He's not looking so good. And Raia, see if you can find any maps of Tangoria. We may need them."

Raia and Olly nodded and gently guided Tommy through the door.

TOMMY STARTLED AWAKE WHEN THE DOOR TO THEIR room burst open a little over an hour later.

"We just missed the thief! I'm sure of it," exclaimed Horatio as he rushed into the room. "Has the prince returned?"

Raia looked up from the guidebook she had been reading and shook her head.

"What do they think happened?" asked Tommy, jumping up from his bed with renewed energy. Olly had brewed a solution from several of the herbs and powders in his knapsack to ease Tommy's throbbing mouth and aching stomach. Tommy felt much better after his short nap.

"They say the fruits on the trees and vines are no longer safe to eat. Salty foods are now sour, and bitter foods are now sweet. The juice of some fruits has turned poisonous, and many people are ill!" Horatio said in a rush. "Also there are swarms of flying insects everywhere. That tree where you picked the berry, Olly—it's covered with hundreds of small orange beetles! The people I spoke to were shocked when I told them we thought the pearl might have been stolen. They kept saying—" Someone knocked on the door. "Oh! That must be the prince!"

Horatio opened the door, and Alexander marched through. He sat down heavily and put his head in his hands, muttering, "I must think. I must think."

"What did you learn, Your Highness?" Horatio asked anxiously.

Alexander lifted his head. "I finally located the pearl thief."

"And . . . ?"

"The pearl has indeed been stolen. I met with the pearl guard, and his wife told me there were rumors of a mysterious person near the border of Amorray." Raia looked up from her book and gazed at the prince intently.

"I am worried Violet is in danger. We must return to the palace as soon as possible!"

"But the thief couldn't have gotten very far, could he? Maybe they should put guards at the village border? You could order that, couldn't you?" suggested Olly.

"Yes, yes!" Tommy said. "And we should search the village. Maybe the thief is hiding close by."

Raia rose and tapped Olly on the shoulder, then said a few words. Olly nodded. "Your Highness? Raia suggests that Tommy speak to the pearl guard and go to where the pearl is kept." He turned back to Raia. "She says . . . really, he can do that? Tommy, you can do that?" Raia nodded.

Tommy looked from Raia to Olly. "What? What can I do?"

"Raia says you might be able to sense the pearl thief's plan by just being in the presence of where he was . . . since it was just stolen . . . Really? I didn't know you could do that!"

Tommy coughed and shot Raia a look. "Uh . . . it only works if it's *right* after. I mean, minutes . . ."

"There's nothing further to be learned there," replied the prince firmly. "It's been hours. Unless we can be *sure* Tommy will learn something, we are just wasting time."

Horatio paced back and forth. "If only we had gotten here sooner. We should never have had those House Specialties!"

"Yes, those can really knock you out," Alexander murmured absentmindedly as he pored over a map.

Tommy's eyes widened. He looked around the room. It appeared that only he had heard what the prince had said. *So the prince knew what effect the drinks would have on us. But that doesn't make sense! Not when we are in a race to catch the pearl thief.* He had to talk to Raia.

"So what do we know?" Horatio continued. "There are no more lands to run to. No more pearls. Where could the thief be going?"

While Horatio and Olly joined the prince in looking for routes the pearl thief might have taken, Tommy crept closer to Raia, trying to catch her attention privately. He cleared his throat quietly and, when she met his eye, motioned toward the door. She nodded.

But just then Horatio called, "Tommy, could you hand me my pipe and tobacco? They're in my brown bag next to the desk chair."

Alexander looked up and saw Raia writing in the book. "Have you found something that could be useful, Raia?" he asked. She closed the book quickly and shook her head.

"I didn't know you smoked, Horatio," Tommy said quickly, trying to distract Alexander. The image of his grandfather popped into his head. For as long as Tommy could remember, Grandpa had smoked a different pipe each day and always left at least four in any one ashtray. "My mom is always telling my grandpa that it's bad for him and makes the house smell awful."

"You have a mother and father?" the prince asked curiously. "Are they also magicians?"

"They have their powers, if that's what you mean," grumbled Tommy. Horatio raised his eyebrows at Tommy and cleared his throat.

"Do you enjoy a pipe, Your Highness?"

Alexander glanced again at Raia, then turned his attention back to Horatio. "Yes, I do."

"Would you care to join me?"

The prince shook his head. "I would certainly accept—if only I had my pipe."

"Ah, well, I just bought one before . . . all this . . ." Horatio flung out his arms and waved them around. Then he jumped up from his chair and shuffled through his bags. "I've been meaning to use it. . . . Here." In the palm of his hand he displayed a handsomely carved pipe. "My prince, I'd be honored if you would be the first to smoke it."

Alexander smiled. "It would be my privilege."

Horatio took some tobacco from his pouch, but Alexander stopped him. "I only smoke one kind of tobacco, Sir Horatio. Only one," he said. He retrieved a checkered pouch from his jacket pocket and filled the pipe with his own special tobacco. "Try some yourself."

Horatio filled his own pipe and then lit both. He and the prince inhaled slowly. Horatio leaned back and closed his eyes. Designs of milky white smoke played in the air.

Tommy swiveled around. The sweet odor tickled his nostrils and reminded him of something—something he had smelled before. He observed Horatio and Alexander side by side. Poor Horatio looked so sickly and pallid compared to the prince, who was wearing a beautifully styled jacket shaded with hints of blue and green. Tommy broke into a cold sweat.

I need to talk to Raia. Now.

As if she could hear his thoughts, Raia stood up. She walked past Tommy, knocking into him. Startled, he looked up and saw her slip the guidebook she had been reading into his satchel, which was hanging on the doorknob. She opened the door.

The prince looked over at her. "Where are you off to, Raia?"

She reddened and mouthed a few words to Olly. She gave the prince an embarrassed smile and slipped out into the hallway.

"Raia is going to the . . . uh . . . toilet," explained Olly. Eager for a change of topic, he added, "We forgot to tell the prince about what we heard at Pubstin!"

"What did we hear?" Horatio said, preoccupied with his pipe.

"You know, about Seraphina and Ezmee seeing the man at the intersection."

While Olly recounted the conversation to Horatio and the prince, Tommy slid the book out of his satchel. A blank piece of paper marked a page where the words *pearl guard* and *she* were circled. The blank paper, he realized, came from the invisible-ink pad. Keeping an eye on the others, he slipped out a pen and shone its light over the page.

A. said guard a man. Meet downstairs now.

He placed the book back in his satchel and announced, abruptly, "I'm going to check on the mulions." He headed for the door.

"What's the matter, my young magician?" he heard the prince ask.

"Nothing. I just want to make sure they have enough water." He hurried out of the room.

Raia was waiting for him at the innkeeper's desk at the bottom of the stairs. The innkeeper looked up from his books and smiled.

"What are you two up to?" he asked.

Tommy looked at Raia. Her eyes glanced at the rack of keys. He knew what she wanted: the key to Alexander's room. How could they get it?

Just then, the front door swung open behind him.

"Yoo hoo," trilled a shrill voice. Tommy spun around to see a tiny, plump woman bustling toward them, her head almost fully concealed by a wide-brimmed straw hat with large floppy flowers pinned to the front. "You are the innkeeper, are you not? My husband and I need help with our baggage."

"I'm sorry, ma'am," the innkeeper said, "but there's no one here to help right now. I'm by myself."

"Well, I never! That is unacceptable! How are we supposed to bring our bags in? We need assistance!" Her voice grew louder, and the innkeeper heaved a sigh. "I'm sorry, ma'am, but . . ."

As the innkeeper and the woman argued, Raia kicked Tommy's shin.

"Ow!" said Tommy, "what'd you do that for?" Raia pointed from herself to Tommy and then at the innkeeper. Tommy's eyes lit up. "Got it," he whispered.

Tommy tapped the innkeeper, who turned to him. "Sir, my . . . uh . . . sister and I can watch the desk for you."

The innkeeper winked at Tommy and Raia and mouthed, "Thank you." He turned to the woman. "Now, ma'am, *of course* I'll carry the bags," he said, and he followed her outside.

Moments later, the woman bounced through the door again, followed by the innkeeper and a thin, nervous man. Both men were laden with large bundles.

"Give me the key to room eight, young lady," he instructed. "There should be two of them. And make sure the lady signs the guest register." The innkeeper nodded at the thick book on the desk and then said, "Come along, Mr. Dibbet. This way."

Raia opened the register and gave it to Mrs. Dibbet. She then retrieved the key.

"Should I sign *my* name," clucked the woman, "or should I sign Dobney's name? Or does it really matter? I do so hate making decisions. How shall I ever decide? My name or Dobney's name?"

"Why not Dobney's name?" Tommy suggested.

Mrs. Dibbet glared at Tommy. "You are a very rude little boy. My Dobney is Mr. Dibbet to the likes of you." She signed the register, snatched the key out of Raia's hand, and wobbled off.

Raia flipped the register around, and they scanned down the list of names. There was the prince's signature and room number. Tommy let out the breath he had been holding.

"Exactly," he said. "But we need to be sure." Raia nodded. Tommy replaced the registration book and turned to the key rack. There, on a hook, hung the second key to Alexander's room. Glancing cautiously around, he slipped it into his right pants pocket. He could feel his heart beating faster and faster.

When the innkeeper returned, he thanked Tommy and Raia for their help. They smiled and then raced upstairs. They had just turned a corner when they came face to face with Olly, nearly knocking him over. He was holding a lantern in one hand and a coat in the other.

"Tommy! I thought you'd be at the stables. And Raia, I thought you were in the bathroom!"

"What are *you* doing here?" asked Tommy.

"Well, it's cold out and I thought you might want your jacket. Actually, it was Prince Alexander who suggested it. He seemed very concerned. Are you already on your way back to the room?"

"Not yet. We . . . uh . . . were delayed. Helping out the innkeeper with some guests." Raia nodded.

"Then I'm not too late after all! Here's your coat. Raia, are you coming back?"

Raia shook her head and pointed to Tommy.

"Ah, I see. Well okay . . . I guess." He looked from Tommy, who was rubbing his palms nervously on his pants, to Raia, who was biting her lip. "What's going on here?" he asked warily. "Are you two up to something? Is it that itch, Tommy?"

Tommy hesitated. He didn't know what to say.

"Tommy, tell me this instant. I might be able to help. Haven't I proven by now that I'm more than just a color guard?"

"Yes, you have," Tommy said seriously. "But Olly, we need you to go back."

Olly shook his head, disappointed.

"Look, Olly, we need you to make sure Horatio and Alexander don't get suspicious so that we have time to . . . to check some things out. That's really important. As important as what we'll be doing."

Olly's eyes lit up. "I see. I can do that. But . . . but what is this all about?"

"The House Specialty. He knew," Tommy said hurriedly. "Plus the smell. First when we were in Amorray, then when Seraphina said she smelled something, and now Alexander's tobacco—and Olly, he's in color!"

"I don't understand."

"We just don't trust him."

"Who?"

"Alexander," Tommy answered, stamping his foot impatiently. "Olly, we really don't have much time. You need to trust me. I'm a wizard, remember? Horatio brought me here to solve this, and that's what I'm doing."

Raia pointed to the lantern Olly was holding. Tommy nodded and said, "Can I take that?" And without giving his friend a chance to respond, Tommy grabbed the lantern and started down the hall toward Alexander's room.

Raia turned to Olly and mouthed, "Book. Tommy's bag." Then she hurried after Tommy.

Olly looked at her helplessly. "You can . . . count on me!" he called out into the empty hallway. Then he slowly turned around and headed back to their room at the opposite end.

WHEN TOMMY AND RAIA REACHED ALEXANDER'S ROOM, Tommy looked both ways down the hall. Seeing no one, he retrieved the key from his pocket, turned it in the lock, and tried the doorknob. The door creaked open.

As soon as they were inside, Tommy closed the door behind them and set the lantern on a table. He took a chair from across the room and angled it so its back snuggled neatly under the doorknob. If everything worked as it did in the movies, no one would be able to enter—even with a key. The lantern's dim glow cut through the darkness of the room. Heavy curtains shut out all but a few beams of the rising moons, and a soft hiss of wind sounded through a window just cracked open.

Tommy and Raia glanced around the room. The prince's coat was draped over the bed beside a small bag. Raia opened the bag and shuffled through its compartments. Tommy, meanwhile, lifted up the coat and felt inside the pockets. Nothing.

Tommy looked dejectedly around the room, thinking, *Maybe our suspicions were all wrong.* He threw the coat down, and as it landed, he heard the sound of two hard objects knocking against each other. The coat must have hit the desk. But what had made the noise?

"Wait a second—" started Tommy, a little louder than he intended. Raia tapped him on the arm and put her finger to her lips. Then she turned to search the desk, pulling out each drawer.

Tommy picked up the coat a second time and glided his fingers over the hem. Along one side he found a long tear in the lining, just large enough for a few fingers and what felt like, and indeed was, a pipe. He fished it out and examined it. The bowl was filled with fresh tobacco.

Raia came up and peered over his shoulder. Tommy slowly turned the pipe upside down and beat the bowl into the palm of his hand, just as he'd seen his grandfather do many times. First, the top layer of tobacco leaves flew out. The rest were packed tightly at the bottom. So he poked his finger in as far as it would go, swirled it around, and tapped the pipe against his palm once more. This time a whole clump of tobacco dropped into his hand, and after it a perfectly round, milk-white pearl. Raia gasped. Tommy stared down at the iridescent gem, unsure of what to do or where to go.

At that moment, keys jingled and the lock turned. The door jiggled against the chair. It had to be Alexander. Tommy glanced helplessly at Raia. There were few places to hide. He drew the curtains and looked out the window. The room was too high up, and they would hurt themselves if they tried to jump. Raia tried the closet, but it was locked. The chair that jammed the lock scraped as it slid out of place.

This is a WWJJD moment, Tommy realized. *What would Jake Jones do?*

He pushed Raia behind the window curtains and closed them. Then he raced to the other side of the bed, turned off the lantern, and ducked down. The door clattered open. Light from the hallway flooded the room, and a tall figure stood silhouetted at the threshold.

Tommy Learns a Lesson

Alexander pushed the fallen chair away from the door. He gazed around the room and saw the pipe and tobacco leaves scattered across the bed. Tommy crouched down as low as he could, but as Alexander strode toward the bed, he realized it wouldn't be low enough. Tommy made a dash for the door, hoping to catch Alexander off guard.

Although Alexander was taken by surprise, he caught Tommy by the shoulders and at the same time kicked the door shut with the heel of his foot. He swiveled Tommy around and grabbed hold of his wrists, frowning at the boy's tightly closed fists.

"Open them," Alexander ordered.

Tommy shook his head, but the prince squeezed his wrists so hard Tommy's eyes watered. Slowly his fingers

142

uncurled, and Alexander let go of one wrist long enough to grab the pearl.

"Playing detective, Mr. Tuddleby," he said, smiling.

"Y-you've lied to us," stammered Tommy. "You're the pearl thief!"

"Have *you* spoken the truth?" Alexander sneered, pushing Tommy backward onto the bed. "You aren't a magician. You may have fooled those simpletons, but I am not so easily deceived."

"Why are you doing this?"

Alexander's stare pierced through him. "Be silent," he ordered. Alexander looked around. "Where's your friend?"

"What friend?"

"What's-her-name," Alexander said impatiently. "The mute girl. Where is she?"

Tommy swallowed. "Wh-when I left the room, I saw her coming out of the bathroom. She said she . . . she was going to check on the m-mulions."

Alexander hauled Tommy over to the window by one arm.

"Where *is* she?" Alexander growled. He shoved one of the curtains aside and pointed across the inn courtyard to the stable.

"You're . . . you're a real . . . creep!" Tommy declared, trying to back away from the other curtain and Raia, who was hiding behind it. "Why are you *doing* this?" he repeated, hoping to distract Alexander.

"I will not answer the accusations of an ordinary child."

"Are you sure that's all I am?" challenged Tommy.

Alexander laughed and pulled Tommy back toward the bed.

"Come now. Do you expect me to believe you're a wizard? You have no magical power. I thought maybe, just maybe, you did. Until the fire, that is."

"The fire?" Tommy looked up, startled. "You caused that? But all those people . . . so many were hurt."

"I didn't start it, but I did make it worse," Alexander said almost gleefully. "I needed to find out—find out *for sure* if you were a wizard. So I added some spark, shall we say." His smile was eerie. "It was quite glorious. And I *knew* that silly little man would think you should be able to do something, so I waited . . . and let it worsen . . . and then I made it all"—he snapped his fingers—"disappear. And you had no choice, did you, but to take credit for it." Alexander growled and then spat, "Something. You. Know. You. Didn't. Do."

"But how could you have stolen the pearls in Rolokon and Tacitonia?" Tommy asked. "They were both missing by the time you arrived. . . ." Tommy hoped Raia was listening and could report back to Horatio and Olly.

The prince smirked. "You're not as clever as you seem, little magician."

"You must have stolen the pearl *before* you arrived at the palace," Tommy said slowly. "And because your father had just died, it made sense for you to return when you did, didn't it?" He looked up.

"Yes, my noble father. The one who stole the kingdom from my hands and gave it away to my undeserving sister."

"Why shouldn't she have it?"

"It is my birthright!" blazed Alexander. "I am the son and firstborn. But Father believed Violet was more fit to be the ruler of Aesteron."

"But you must have lost color like everyone else. How did you get it back?" Tommy asked, hoping to calm Alexander's temper.

"Do you think me an ordinary person?" the prince snapped. "With each pearl, my powers strengthened. I gained control. Now, with all four, I have power over *everything*." His face twisted into an ugly sneer.

"But the pearl of Tacitonia . . . that went missing while you were still in Rolokon."

The man's lips curled into an eerie smile. "They were fools. The pearl guard had only mislaid the pearl."

"So you found it before anyone knew and just didn't say anything—"

"Enough!" the prince hissed. "By returning, I cleared myself. Everyone believes in me. If it weren't for you . . ." He leaned over Tommy and bore down on the boy's shoulders.

"You have caused me great trouble, and I have spoken too much."

"Then why not let me go?" Tommy winced from the pain. "You have the pearls. What can I do?"

"No one else must know of my new strength until we reach the mountain. There, no one can conquer me."

"We? I'm going with you?"

"Do you think I would be so foolhardy as to leave you here? You'd warn them. Either you come with me, or I see to you now." Without waiting for Tommy's response, Alexander yanked Tommy up from the bed. "Collect the bags."

WITHIN TWENTY MINUTES THEY HAD LOADED UP Alexander's horse. Tommy cringed with Alexander's every word and resisted every shove forward. As they left, Alexander had scanned the room. The curtain moved ever so slightly, and Tommy held his breath, but Alexander simply grabbed his last bag and pulled Tommy out the door. Just as they turned the corner, Tommy thought he saw Raia slip out of the room and head the other direction.

She should have gotten help by now, he thought. *Where could she be?*

The prince tied Tommy's hands together, heaved him into the saddle, and strapped his bindings to the saddle.

"Why can't I ride my mulion?" asked Tommy.

"Because you'll try to escape, and my horse is faster. She'll throw you off if you should attempt to ride her alone," warned Alexander. "By the way, I left a note for your dear friends saying I needed your magical services immediately and will contact them soon. They trust me and will not question my wishes."

Tommy hoped that by now that wasn't true, but no rescue party arrived.

The prince mounted the horse and urged the animal down the road. Tommy nearly fell off—he grasped the prince's coattail before he slid off entirely. For the first time, through the darkness, Tommy noticed the glowing colors of the ring on Alexander's finger.

FOR SEVERAL HOURS THEY FOLLOWED THE WINDING riverbanks, leaving the lowlands of Tangoria far behind. Sometime after midnight they stopped by the river falls to let the horse drink. The three moons loomed large and full, so the sky was lit as brightly as if the sun had just risen.

"Could I have some water too?" asked Tommy. He was parched and a little dizzy, having eaten nothing since tasting the poisonous berry.

"Off the horse," Alexander ordered, unstrapping him from the saddle. With his hands still tied, Tommy slid to the ground and landed on his butt. Alexander roughly pulled him to his feet and steered him up a hill with a hand at the back of his neck.

"You think you're so clever, little magician." Alexander's fingers dug into Tommy's skin as he pushed

Tommy forward. "You think you can outsmart me? A boy like you? You have no idea. No *idea* what I'm capable of." He stopped Tommy at the edge of a steep drop. "Look."

Tommy took one look at the chasm and closed his eyes. Alexander pulled Tommy's head back and shouted, "*LOOK!*"

From the clifftop, Tommy could see all of Tangoria and beyond.

"This is mine," said Alexander. "I rule over all of this."

"I thought Violet ruled over the land," Tommy muttered.

Alexander laughed. "Violet is a foolish woman. She has no idea what it means to have real power."

"You don't have real power," Tommy spat out. "You're just a . . . a . . . a bully."

"Really? That's all you think, is it? The mudslide? The tree that fell on you? You believe these were all accidents?"

"So you *were* there! I thought I saw someone outside the cave."

"Clearly it didn't have the effect I intended. And then the bridge. You were never supposed to reach the other side before it fell apart. But you just kept on," Alexander snarled through gritted teeth. "You have caused me more trouble than you are worth. It's time you learn a lesson you won't forget."

Alexander pushed Tommy along the cliff's edge toward a tree. He raised Tommy's bound wrists and tied them to a low-hanging branch with a strong, thin piece of twine that cut into Tommy's hands.

Alexander stepped back. From a pouch hung around his neck he withdrew a square metal box. From that, he pulled out a jeweled case. Tommy had never seen so many glittering stones: red and green ones and sparkling, translucent gems that looked like diamonds. The prince unclasped the hinge and opened the case to display three milky-white pearls. Delicate gold hooks held the stolen pearls to a velvet cushion, with one set still empty. Alexander set Tangoria's pearl into the unused clasp. Then, closing his eyes, he extended his hand, allowing the moons' beams to glint off the pearls.

At first nothing much happened, although Tommy did feel a bit of a chill. Then he felt rustling at his feet and looked down. To his disbelief, he saw the grass growing at a rapid pace, entwining his feet in thick ropes. The petals of wildflowers spread to an enormous width as their stems grew long.

Tiny insects with hard black shells and spindly legs swelled as large as Tommy's foot. There were more of them than Tommy had ever dreamed. Long, thick branches from the tree Tommy was tied to reached out toward him, leaves flapping like huge, grasping hands. Over it all he could hear Alexander's gloating cackle.

Tommy had never wanted to run so much in his life, but he was trapped. The insects surrounded him, and clouds of flower pollen engulfed him. Everything seemed to hiss and screech at once.

"Stop!" Tommy hollered. "Stop all this! I can't breathe!"

The prince enjoyed Tommy's panic a bit longer before clasping shut the case of pearls. Within seconds, everything returned to normal.

"The demonstration is over," Alexander said. "I believe I've made my point."

Tommy shook off the pollen and cleared his lungs. One thing he knew: wildflowers and tufts of grass would never seem so harmless to him again.

Alexander freed Tommy from the branch and thrust a canteen of water at him, ordering, "Drink."

Tommy grabbed the canteen and drank thirstily. The prince took it back, and Tommy wiped his mouth awkwardly with the back of one of his tied hands.

Then Alexander pushed Tommy roughly back toward the horse, heaved him on top, and again strapped him securely to the saddle.

"Stay there, and don't give me any trouble," Alexander warned. "Or do. I'm sure it would be entertaining." Then he took a few steps down the riverbank.

Moments later, Tommy heard a faint trill of a bird from a distance. Something about it caught his attention. A few seconds later he heard it again. And then again. It came at regular intervals . . . but now it had stopped. Alexander was close to the rushing water, filling the canteen, and did not seem to have noticed.

Am I imagining it? Tommy thought. He closed his eyes to concentrate and heard the trilling again. Barely audible. Then twice more, in the same pattern. It sounded familiar.

Of course! My whistle! When you pushed down on a little button and blew, it made a bird call. His friends must be near. He didn't dare look too obviously toward the sound, but he raised his hands as high above his head as he could reach and moved them back and forth like a windshield wiper.

"What are you doing?" Alexander was climbing the bank, securing the canteen's lid.

"S-s-stretching," Tommy stammered.

"What?" Alexander barked as he mounted the horse.

"Stretching," Tommy said loudly. "My arms. They're cramping up." Tommy lowered his hands. He wasn't sure how far away his friends were, but maybe they had seen him.

AT THE FOOT OF THE TALLEST MOUNTAIN IN THE LAND, Alexander dismounted, leaving Tommy still bound to the saddle. Here, the Collos River curled away from the main road, and although the current was rapid, the river seemed narrower. Tommy remembered learning in school that smaller springs and streams often flowed into a river, making it larger and more powerful as it flowed down through the mountains. They must be closer to its source, then.

They struck out uphill, off the road, Alexander leading the horse. They paused a couple of times to rest. When they had climbed over two-thirds of the way toward the mountaintop, Alexander lifted his arm and curled his hand into a fist. Although the sun was barely visible above the horizon, a ray of light, as if pulled by sheer force of will, struck the stone of his ring.

Soon Tommy heard the clip of a horse's hooves. A stunning silver-and-gold-striped stallion appeared. On it sat a young man dressed in a plain brown tunic, his pale face covered in freckles, his rust-red hair frizzed out in all directions. Alexander murmured instructions that Tommy couldn't hear. The boy transferred Alexander's baggage to the silver horse. Then he led the black-and-white horse—with Tommy still on it—up a narrow path to one side, while Alexander led the other horse straight up the mountainside.

"What's your name?" asked Tommy after a few silent minutes.

The boy did not respond. Was he a servant? Tommy wondered whether, like Raia, he came from Tacitonia. "Can you talk?"

He turned slowly toward Tommy, as if in a trance, and said, "Elias."

"Can I have something to drink, Elias? I'm so thirsty."

"You will drink when we reach Rhian."

Rhian! That's the place Olly mentioned that one night, Tommy thought, excited. *And it's the place in the* Book of Eldred. *The magical place. It's real!*

"Rhian? What's that?" Tommy asked, hoping to coax more information from him.

Elias did not respond.

"But what's up there? What are we going to do?"

"I'm to take you to the great hall."

The ground leveled off, and the servant mounted the horse, sitting behind Tommy, and concentrated on the path ahead of them. As they climbed, everything around them seemed to change. They were surrounded first by rows of trees, then open fields, then more trees. There was a wild grace in the unruly tangle of branches, and the grasses grew a foot high. Flowers blossomed in every color, and a deep purple hue, uninterrupted by even a thin shadow of gray or white, painted the sky a lustrous, even tone.

"Is that it?" Tommy exclaimed as a large mansion appeared among the trees.

Elias nodded.

"This place is more beautiful than the palace—but I can't really explain why. I mean, the palace is so wonderful, yet . . ." Tommy frowned thoughtfully.

"The palace," observed the servant, "is not enchanted."

The Great Escape

They stopped at the edge of the small clearing around the mansion. Tommy saw a thin channel of water disappearing through the trees.

"We are about to enter the great hall. I must blindfold you," Elias informed Tommy.

"You don't have—"

But before he could finish, Tommy felt a thick cloth being wrapped tightly around his eyes.

"Do not speak again," ordered Elias.

The horse stopped, and Elias jumped to the ground. He unstrapped Tommy and gripped him under the arms. "Swing your feet around to your right and jump. I won't let you go."

Tommy did as he was told. He heard the crunch of pine needles as his feet hit the earth. The young man led Tommy forward by the arm, catching him as he stumbled over hidden bulges of soil and stones. Soon there was a hard, smooth surface beneath his shoes, and he heard a door being unlocked. It opened, and they entered.

"Watch yourself on the stairs," warned Elias as he prodded Tommy along. Unable to see, with his hands still tied, Tommy felt, for the first time, that he had no control over anything. The steps creaked unsteadily beneath them, and a dingy, stale odor drifted up from below. At the bottom of the staircase, Tommy listened to the echo of their footsteps against what must be a stone floor and walls. The air was musty, cold, and damp.

After a while, they stopped again. Tommy heard the scrape of a key in a lock. A latch slid across and a bolt unclicked. A door opened. The servant shoved Tommy forward, closed the door behind him, and secured it.

Alone, Tommy listened to Elias's footsteps receding into the distance. Until he untied the ropes that bound his hands, he wouldn't be able to remove the blindfold, which was knotted tightly at the back of his head. So he walked until he bumped into a wall and then slowly lowered himself to the stone floor, supporting his back against the cool stone. He twisted his wrists and wriggled his fingers around the already worn rope. Eventually one coil loosened, and with a little more work, his hands were free.

Tommy loosened the knot and tore off the blindfold. He looked around him and for a few seconds saw only a pitch-black emptiness. He froze, paralyzed with fear. Had Alexander blinded him so he would never see again? How could he free himself? Would his friends ever find him? After a few anxious moments, Tommy realized he was not blind at all. The room was just *very* dark. He calmed down, and soon he made out the dim outlines of several tables and what looked like large washing basins.

Doesn't look like a dungeon to me, he thought. *Looks like they stuck me in the laundry room. There's got to be a way out of this.*

Very much relieved, he settled down to devise his escape . . . but instead drifted off to sleep, exhausted from the long night of travel.

WHEN TOMMY AWOKE, HIS MUSCLES HAD STIFFENED IN the dank chill, and he was very hungry, having not eaten for nearly a day. The room wasn't quite as dark as before: a bit of late-morning light crept in through a small window near the ceiling. He rose slowly to his feet. The room wasn't large at all and was cluttered with all sorts of odds and ends.

Be methodical, Jake Jones always says. Methodical and persistent. No problem.

First he inspected the perimeter carefully—twice in fact—and then examined the items on the tables to see if any could be useful. One table was piled high with boxes. He pulled them off one by one, hoping to find some kind of useful tool, but they were all empty. Behind them, though . . .

As he pulled down more boxes, a door frame became visible, blocked off by the table. Excited, Tommy dragged the table away and turned the knob. It was locked. But the door was not very sturdy. The wood had softened with the dampness of the room, and the lock was rusted. Tommy tried the knob again, pushing at the same time.

"Who's there?" cried a very muffled voice.

Tommy jumped back, shocked. *Who else is here? Are they working with Alexander?* This was his only escape route, though, so no matter the consequences, it was worth taking the chance.

"Could you help me open this door?" he called out. "Maybe from your side, you'll—"

"I've tried," answered the voice. "It's hopeless."

"Well, maybe if we both work together, it won't be," he argued. "You pull while I push." Tommy pushed as hard as he could. Then he stepped back and rammed his shoulder against the door once . . . twice . . . three times. At the fourth, the door jerked open and Tommy flew into another room, barely catching himself from falling flat on his stomach.

"Are you all right? Who are you?"

Tommy swung around. This room was pitch black, with no windows at all. In the dim light from the open door he could barely make out the face of a woman.

"I guess I'm fine," he answered, rubbing his shoulder. "And my name is Tommy. What are *you* doing here?"

"I have been imprisoned in this chamber for many days. You may call me Eleyna. Who brought you here, Tommy?"

"Why should I tell you a thing?" he demanded. "How do I know you aren't evil too?"

"Alexander brought you, didn't he?"

Tommy looked sharply at the woman. "What do you know about him?"

Eleyna did not respond.

Tommy didn't know what to make of this woman, but she certainly wasn't helping matters. "If you know what's going on here, I'd appreciate your telling me. I got stuck in this whole mess by accident! I didn't ask to come here and chase after any pearl stealers. They just thought I was someone I wasn't. At least, I'm not. Not that I'm not someone," he added, growing flustered. "But I'm not the someone they thought I was."

"You are quite right, Tommy. I'm not being very helpful. I know much, but there is little I can do, especially if Alexander has stolen the pearls of which you speak."

"Why is that? Who are you?"

Eleyna stepped into the doorway between the two rooms. With better light he could see she wore a simple robe, and her long hair flowed down her back.

"First, tell me of your journey, and of Alexander." Then, noting Tommy's hesitation, she added, "Please, trust me."

Perhaps it was the sadness in her eyes or the urgency in her voice or the reassurance of her smile, but he did just that. They sat in the open doorway so they could hear if anyone approached Tommy's room. And while Tommy told of his travels and how Olly and Horatio thought he was a magician, and how Raia knew he wasn't, and how Alexander was the pearl thief, the mysterious woman listened in silence.

TOMMY HAD JUST FINISHED HIS STORY WHEN FOOTSTEPS sounded in the hallway outside. They closed the door between them, and Tommy pushed the table back, dashed to one corner, and lowered his head. He could only hope it was dim enough that his visitor would not notice the loosened ropes, the untied kerchief, or empty boxes scattered on the floor.

The door opened.

"Here is some food." It was Elias. "Would you like me to bring it over to you? If you want to eat, I'll have to untie your ropes." He waited several seconds. "Answer me."

"You can leave it where you are," Tommy replied acidly.

The servant shrugged his shoulders. "Very well," he said, and closed the door behind him.

Relieved that he hadn't been discovered, Tommy collected the food and reopened the door to Eleyna's chamber. "That guy is so strange!"

Eleyna stiffened. "What guy? What did he look like?"

"Red hair. Freckles. But that's not what's so strange. He just acts weird. Like he's a robot. Do you know him?"

Eleyna took in a quick breath.

"Are you okay?" asked Tommy.

"What? Yes. Yes, of course," she replied with a small smile. She appeared lost in thought for a few seconds but then abruptly cleared her throat and nodded toward the meal Elias had brought. "You should eat something."

Tommy looked down. "Do you want any?"

"No, I am fine. It is your food."

It was a simple meal of soup and hard, crusty bread. Tommy filled his spoon with broth and allowed the liquid to trickle down to his stomach. It was surprisingly good. He already felt much better. But before he could take another bite, a key scraped at Tommy's door. Elias was back!

Once more, Tommy closed the door between them. Realizing he wouldn't have time to move the table back in place, he frantically threw boxes on top of it to at least partially hide the door. He then raced back to the dark corner where Elias had left him. This time, however, he heard something more: furious whisperings as the lock was tried several times but did not open.

At last, the door opened softly and then shut again.

"Is—is anyone h-h-here?" stammered a familiar, nervous voice.

Tommy rose. "Olly? Olly, is that you?"

"Tommy! He's here!" Olly whispered excitedly. He stumbled through the darkness, followed by Raia and Horatio, and embraced Tommy. Raia also gave him a hug, which surprised them both.

"How did you find me?"

"You have Raia to thank," replied Horatio. "Back at the inn, Alexander left us to look for you, and Olly told me what Raia had said about the book and Tommy's bag. We checked that out and saw the page she marked—"

"—and Tommy, you mentioned that Alexander had color," added Olly. "Which made no sense—"

"Then we ran into Raia, who told us everything, and the innkeeper showed us Alexander's note. . . . Oh, I really didn't want to believe it!"

"But he did," Olly added. "We followed you, and we saw what the prince did to you with the tree." He shuddered.

Horatio shook his head sadly. "We couldn't follow you or the prince into this place, so we followed the river to the cave where it begins, intending to hide and make a plan. Then Olly found a trapdoor in the cave, and it led to a tunnel that brought us here."

"As it turns out, Raia is very good at picking locks!" Olly added, smiling proudly at her. Raia rolled her eyes but returned his smile appreciatively.

"Anyway, we can tell you the rest later," said Horatio as he pulled Tommy toward the door. "We really must go."

"I can't," protested Tommy. "Not without Eleyna."

Horatio released his arm. "Who, may I ask, is she?"

"She's being held prisoner in the next room. She has to come with us." He opened the door and said, "Eleyna, it's okay—my friends found us and they can get us out of here!"

Eleyna stepped out, and Tommy introduced her to everyone.

"So, you came through the tunnel from the spring?" she said. At their nods, she continued, "I had completely forgotten about it. Long ago, before we installed pipes, the kitchen staff used it to bring water from the river directly to the kitchen and laundry."

"Have you lived here for many years?" asked Horatio, studying her closely.

"I lived here when I was a child."

Olly glanced at Horatio. Tommy wondered what they were thinking.

Raia pulled at Olly's jacket. Olly nodded and said, "Raia says it's time we stop talking and get out of here before dark."

Horatio took out his pocket watch, and worry creased his brow. "Blow! My watch stopped. Tommy, what time is it?"

Tommy shook his head and showed the wristband to Horatio. "I told you before: this isn't a watch."

"Your world uses the same symbols we do!" remarked Olly, pushing Tommy toward the door. "How interesting! But it's time to *leave*."

"What?" Tommy asked, shaking Olly's hand away and staring at the symbols. "My world doesn't use these symbols. And it's not a watch!"

"You might be a wizard, Thomas Tuddleby, but I know a watch when I see one!" insisted Olly as he herded them all out the door and down the hall outside.

"*Tuddleby?*" Eleyna said. "Your name is *Thomas Tuddleby?* Who did you say gave this to you?"

"My uncle. A couple of months ago. Before he left." They reached a door, and Olly waved them to a halt before slipping through it.

"Did he tell you anything about it?" she asked anxiously.

"He said it was the answer to all my problems and a whole lot more, which is true because—"

"He said nothing else?" she interrupted. Olly returned and waved for them to follow him.

Tommy frowned. "No, and I don't see why it's so—"

Eleyna cut him off. "We must go to the cave immediately."

"We *are* going to the cave, if you would all please keep moving," Olly chided, sounding frustrated. They followed him into a dusty, abandoned kitchen with rusted sinks and a few cobwebbed pots.

"I thought you said we couldn't do anything as long as Alexander had the pearls," Tommy reminded Eleyna.

"I- I just remembered something."

"Would you care to share with us what that something is?" said Horatio.

"Horatio!" scolded Tommy. "I'm sure Eleyna knows what she's doing."

"After Alexander, I'm not sure who I can believe in," said Horatio, eyeing Eleyna icily.

She ignored him. "We must hurry, or we'll be too late. Raia, please take my hand. I have been in the darkness too long. For the time being, I need you to guide me."

The Seed of Rhian

Olly led them to a small wooden door that opened into a musty, dank tunnel. Horatio retrieved two lanterns they had brought and handed one to Olly. They stepped into the darkness. The light flickered over the silky spiderweb designs that veiled the walls, and the tapping sound of their footsteps echoed along the stone. At times the ceiling was so low that they all had to hunch over—even Horatio—and Eleyna lagged behind, even with Raia's aid.

Horatio sighed and said to Eleyna, "Why don't you try walking alone? Your eyes should have adjusted to this dim light by now."

"They have not," she retorted indignantly. "I still can't see clearly."

"Is it that you can't see clearly, or that you can't see at all?" Olly murmured.

They all stopped, startled. Eleyna loosened her grip on Raia.

"Please, Sir Horatio, Olly, you must trust me."

"We're not going any farther until you tell us who you are," Horatio said sternly.

Eleyna shook her head. "I haven't time to explain. Not here. Not now. You must understand, I am the only one who can save the kingdom. Please let me do so." She pushed Raia forward, and the rest of them, reluctantly, followed.

The tunnel grew wider and the ceilings higher. Tommy stopped and peered past the light of the lantern Horatio held. "What's that squeaking noise?" he asked.

"Shh! It's probably a bat. Be quiet, or they'll come down from where they've been sleeping," whispered Horatio.

But it was too late. A furry swarm emerged from the cobwebbed crevices of the tunnel and surrounded them in a cloud. Tommy dropped to the ground. Raia grabbed Eleyna and fled down the dark passageway. Horatio followed.

"Come on, Olly," Tommy urged, rising to a cautious crouch. "Let's get out of here!" But the color guard stood paralyzed amid the flurry of flapping wings. "Olly," Tommy said firmly, unpeeling Olly's trembling fingers from around the lantern handle, "I know you can do this.

You're an adventurer! You've done so many brave things already. This is just one more thing we have to get through."

As if emerging from a trance, Olly focused his eyes on Tommy and nodded. He seized Tommy's arm, and together, they ran. They did not stop until they rejoined the others at the stairs that led to the trapdoor and the cave.

His confidence recovered, Olly climbed up the stairs first. A cool breeze broke through the heavy air of the tunnel as he pushed open the door. Tommy climbed up last, and as he closed the trapdoor, he looked around him. More darkness. But beyond their lantern light, a pinch of sunlight glowed in the distance, and he could hear the soft swish of swirling waters.

"Hear that sound? That's the spring," Olly informed him. "Just follow the light, and we'll soon be there."

"No." Horatio held up his hand, and they all stared at him. He turned toward Eleyna. "I am familiar with the mythologies of Aesteron. They describe an enchanter—the one who distributed the pearls—who lived on top of the highest mountain and protected the kingdom below. Supposedly this enchanter had a granddaughter who was born without sight. But no one ever saw or heard of her— until now." Horatio eyed her closely. "Perhaps it would be more correct to call you the enchantress of Aesteron."

"One might better describe this myth as a well-concealed reality," Eleyna said quietly. "Yes, I am the enchantress."

"But if you're an enchantress, then you must have some powers. Couldn't you have used them to escape?" asked Olly.

"I do have powers," she responded. "But much of my strength comes from the light of the sun, the moon, and the stars. I gain strength from the woods around me, the grass and the soil.

"In that lightless room, I lost the powers that would have allowed me to escape. I can sustain myself for a very long time, but without my ring—"

"You mean the one with the big stone that glows all different colors?" asked Tommy.

"Yes," she answered anxiously. "Do you know where it is?"

"Alexander has it."

"He stole it from you?" pressed Horatio.

Eleyna nodded.

"And it's the ring your grandfather gave you, isn't it? The one that allows you to see, as written in the *Book of Eldred*?"

"Yes," she said, lowering her gaze.

"What does that mean, though?" Olly asked Eleyna. "He can see already. Will the ring give him any powers?"

"The ring allows the wearer to observe whatever he or she wishes—near and far—"

"Is that how Alexander found out where all the pearls were kept?" interrupted Tommy.

Eleyna nodded. "Alexander wants to rule over all, and I am the only person who can stop him. In a chamber below the ground, I was no threat to him. With the pearls and my ring, he believes he will have complete power."

"Doesn't he?"

She did not answer.

"He seems to think the pearls will give him control over everything. Isn't that right?" persisted Tommy.

"The pearls allow the possessor to control the environment—the storms, the heat, the success or failure of the harvest, and much more. With the insight provided by the ring . . ."

". . . he has power over everything," Horatio finished.

The enchantress nodded. "The ring and pearls together are indeed very powerful. But there is one thing that can stop him: the Seed of Rhian."

"Seed?"

"It is the name of the fifth pearl of Colloster." For the first time Eleyna smiled. "At least, my grandfather always called it that."

"So where is it?"

"The spring."

"Does Alexander know about it?"

Eleyna shook her head.

Raia tugged on Eleyna's hand and looked pleadingly at the rest. "Yes," said Eleyna, "we haven't time to waste."

They had gone only a few feet when they heard the mulions whinnying. Tommy ran to them. "You brought Kia with you!" he said, kissing his mulion and hugging her neck. "They must be thirsty. Maybe we should let them drink from the spring."

"After we find this pearl-seed Eleyna was talking about," advised Olly.

At the mouth of the cave, the spring sparkled under the sun's warm rays. The gurgling pool had worn into the stone floor, leaving little room to walk around its edges. On the other side, Tommy saw two thin streams of water flowing out from the cave and merging into one in the woods beyond.

"The Collos rises from this spring. The Seed is also hidden here," explained Eleyna. "Its magical qualities give the other four pearls their own powers."

Tommy's eyes lit up. "So as long as we have the Seed, we can fight Alexander. How can we find it?"

She pointed. "It is over there, in a gold case under that thick stone slab that juts out into the water."

"Thank you, Eleyna," a low voice said. "You have been most helpful." At the other side of the spring, the tall figure of Alexander appeared. Olly gasped fearfully as the prince strode across the cave toward them.

"You were unwise to escape. Even if you were miles away, I would have found you with the ring. No one can escape me—now that I am ruler," the prince gloated.

"But you're not," retorted Tommy. Out of the corner of his eye, he saw Raia edging around the spring toward the slab. He had to keep Alexander's attention off her.

"Foolish boy. Do you need further demonstration of my powers? Now that I know about the Seed—"

"Don't, Alexander," pleaded Eleyna, reaching a hand out to him. "Don't hurt any more people—"

Alexander approached the enchantress and brushed wisps of hair from her face. "You lack the power, Eleyna, and you lack the sight. Even I know you cannot fight that which you cannot see. How will you stop me?"

Tommy glanced toward the spring just as Raia kneeled down and reached under the water. When her hand emerged, she held a shell. A gold shell. Tommy caught Olly's eye, and Olly nodded very slightly. He had seen Raia also.

Olly cleared his throat loudly and strutted toward Alexander, drawing his gaze away from Raia.

Alexander looked startled but jeered, "What? *You* have something to say now? You are incapable of doing *any*thing right, which is how you lost the pearl in the first place. And you are so *stupid* that you actually thought this *child*"—he pointed at Tommy—"could be a wizard."

Olly glared at the prince. "You're wrong. Tommy can fight you. Can't you, Tommy?"

Tommy gulped.

Alexander snickered. "Him? There's nothing magical about him at all. He's nothing."

Horatio turned to Tommy. "Is this true?"

"Enough of this drivel," Alexander snarled, saving Tommy from answering. He turned toward the spring, but Raia had already backed away. "The pearl. That rock looks like a solid piece of the cave floor. You are sure, Eleyna?"

She did not respond.

Suddenly Elias appeared from behind a large rock near the cave wall. "Find the pearl she speaks of," ordered Alexander. He caressed the enchantress's cheek with the back of his hand. "Perhaps, Eleyna, we can rule together— as you once hoped we would. After all, you are my wife." He smiled at Tommy and his companions.

The four adventurers stared, flabbergasted, at Eleyna.

"You married him?" Tommy swallowed. "How could you?"

Eleyna pushed Alexander away from her. "Tommy, you must let me explain."

She stepped forward and tripped. Tommy grabbed her arm. She regained her balance and enclosed his hand within both of hers. In the light, Tommy could now see how pale and thin and young Eleyna was, her flaming hair flowing in waves and curls down her back. "I am older than I look, but it wasn't too long ago that I was as restless as you are now. I was tired of remaining on the mountain. So I decided to explore the kingdom and meet its people. On my journey, I met Alexander and fell in love. We married. He never knew of my powers."

"But I soon found out." The prince smirked. "Didn't you think I would notice you were a witch?"

"I have it." The servant approached Alexander, the gold shell Tommy had seen in Raia's hand now clutched in his.

"Open it," ordered the prince.

"No, Elias!" Eleyna shouted. "Listen to me!"

But the servant unhinged the clasp and opened the shell. Embedded in the casement lay . . . nothing.

Alexander roared, "NO!" He looked from Olly to Tommy, but his eyes settled on Raia, who was retreating further into the shadows. "You! Grab her!" he yelled to Elias.

Raia made a run for it, but Elias lunged at her. They both fell to the ground. He pinned one of her arms behind her and then grabbed the other. She struggled, but Elias used all his strength to pry open her clenched fist. Her palm opened, and Elias grabbed the pearl.

Tommy scrambled across the cave floor and leaped at Elias. Caught off guard, the servant loosened his grip on Raia, who jumped onto his back, throwing him off balance.

Tommy almost missed the glint as Elias staggered and dropped the Seed. He flung himself after it, but missed. It skipped and rolled into a small, dark crevice.

Alexander splashed toward him as he crossed the spring. Elias lunged forward, though Raia caught his tunic and dragged him back.

Eleyna thrust out her hands. Alexander and Elias slammed to a halt, as though they had hit an invisible wall. Raia lost her grip and fell backwards.

Tommy reached for the Seed, but it slid deeper into the narrow crack. *I need a stick or something!* he thought. *Think, think!* He frantically went through his pockets . . . and grinned.

From his pants pocket he peeled out the strand of thick spiderweb and pushed it into the cleft until it stuck to the pearl.

"Got it!" he cried, backing deeper into the shadows of the cave. Raia darted around the stalled prince and joined him.

In his palm lay the largest and most breathtaking of all the pearls. This one had a creamy rose tinge.

Alexander pushed against the invisible wall.

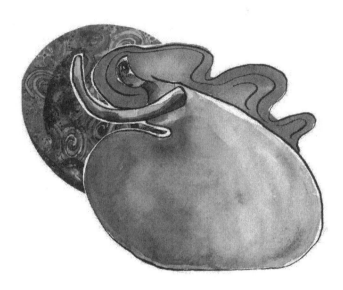

"Come no closer," Eleyna cautioned. "Do not be deceived, Alexander. Even without the pearls and the ring, I am an enchantress. And I am growing stronger now that I am free."

"But I have your ring and the pearls. Even without the Seed, I am more powerful than you can imagine," said the prince with a smirk. He pointed the ring at Eleyna, and she froze; each was now paralyzed in the other's magical grasp. Elias remained still, his expression now vacant.

"What should I do with the pearl?" Tommy called out.

"Your band," Eleyna gasped. "P-pull the knob at the side." Eleyna's outstretched arms trembled. Horatio came up behind Tommy and pointed to the knob.

Tommy pulled it, and the clasp sprung open. Inside lay a small circle of diamonds. "It must go here," Tommy said under his breath. He peeled the pearl out of the sticky web.

"The Seed . . . it's in!" Tommy shouted.

"Hold it out to the sunlight. Hurry!" she pleaded. "I can't hold him much longer."

Tommy dashed to the mouth of the cave and extended the watch into the sun. Rays of light surrounded the pearl with a furious glow.

Eleyna broke from Alexander's hold but then fell to the ground. The earth trembled beneath them. Thick, sooty clouds rushed in like blackened chariots, and the wind hissed around them. Thunder rolled across the sky and crescendoed into a sweeping *C-CRACK*. Pellets of hail shattered around Tommy's feet, and he ducked back into the cave just as lightning splintered the ground where Alexander stood. Licking tongues of fire surrounded him. Another crash of thunder, followed by echoing rumblings, drowned out his cries.

The fire surged upward until the prince disappeared from sight. And then, just as suddenly, the flames dissolved into smoldering ashes. Amid the cinders lay the pearl box and the ring, flashing shades and shades of color. Alexander, however, was gone.

Saying Goodbye

At first there was only silence. They all stood still, dumbstruck by Alexander's sudden disappearance. Only moments ago, all hope for saving the kingdom had seemed lost.

Then a gentle wind rippled the spring pool. The smoky clouds broke and crawled from sight, revealing a brilliant sunset.

Olly stepped out from behind a rock and cleared his throat. "Excuse me, Miss Eleyna, but what happened to the prince? Was he taken away by magical spirits? Or escaped? Or could he be d-dead or something dreadful like that?"

The enchantress had buried her face in her hands. She looked up. "All of those things, Olly," she replied. "The pearls were never meant for evil. When they are exposed to the heat of the sun, their powers are unpredictable, ruled by the possessor's whim. But the Seed is the ultimate protector of all. If only I had realized sooner . . ." Her words trailed off into a somber silence.

Horatio emerged from the shadows. "Don't be so hard on yourself."

She turned her head aside. "He was evil. He was not who I wanted him to be. How could I be so deceived?"

"He was too full of jealousy, Eleyna. You did the only thing you could do," Horatio said firmly. "If it weren't for the Seed and your powers, he would have destroyed the lands. Remember that."

"I thought we were goners!" exclaimed Tommy. He picked up the pearl box and the ring and brought them to the enchantress. "How did those diamonds ever get into my band?"

Eleyna slipped the ring onto her finger and blinked several times. She took a deep breath and exhaled slowly. "The colors. They are so brilliant." She gazed all around until her eyes finally rested on Elias, who was standing apart from the rest, his head lowered.

She approached him and took his hands. "It's not your fault, Eli. I brought him here." He looked up into her eyes, and she embraced him.

Elias clung to her. "I'm so sorry. I didn't know what I was doing. I'm so sorry."

Eleyna stroked the back of his head. "No, I am sorry, dear brother. It's over now," she said soothingly.

"Elias is your brother?" Tommy blurted, though now that they stood side by side, he saw the resemblance: the same fiery red hair, the same eyes.

Eleyna nodded as Elias broke from her embrace and stepped back, wiping his eyes with the sleeve of his tunic. "Alexander took my brother prisoner, placed him under his power, and then used him against me. Eli had no control over his actions. Please do not judge him harshly."

"It . . . it felt like I was buried. Deep within my body," Elias murmured. "I knew what I was doing but couldn't stop myself." He turned to Tommy and grasped his hand. "I'm so sorry. Please forgive me."

Tommy looked up at him and smiled. "Believe me, I saw what Alexander could do. There's nothing to forgive."

"So everything's back to normal?" asked Olly.

Eleyna nodded to Elias, who brought her the gold shell. She placed the Seed of Rhian gently inside and closed it. "I believe you know where this belongs," she said, smiling at him. Elias gave her a rueful look and then walked over to replace it at the mouth of the spring.

"Now that the Seed is back, and we have all the pearls, we can restore each land to its former condition." Eleyna opened the box and handed it to Olly. "Olly, you know what to do, yes?"

"We can do this here?" Olly's eyes widened. "Now?"

"Of course," Eleyna replied. "The water that flows from this spring over the Seed gives the pearls their powers. A very long time ago, there was only the Seed. But my grandfather realized that consolidating all this power in one place, in one thing, was too dangerous. These pearls"—she motioned to them—"were once part of the Seed. My grandfather understood that the lands would be better protected if the power of the Seed was disseminated across the lands."

"That's the story of the messenger! The story you told me, Horatio!" exclaimed Tommy. He paused. "I . . . I wonder . . ." Forgetting where he was, he turned to Eleyna. "Was the messenger my—"

But before he could finish, Eleyna asked, "Do you have what you need, Olly? I'm sure Raia is very anxious to have her voice back." She raised her eyebrows almost imperceptibly at Tommy and mouthed, "Later."

Raia nodded vigorously as Olly retrieved a water dropper from his mulion's pack. He knelt down, filled the dropper with water from the spring, and in quick succession added three droplets to each of the pearls. Within moments, he and Horatio were fully in color, top to bottom.

"What a relief!" Horatio exhaled. "We looked so dreadful without any color!"

Tommy raised his eyebrows, amused. "Uh . . . Horatio . . ." he said, "you may want to broaden your wardrobe choices!" While Olly was dressed in red pants and an olive-green coat, Horatio's clothing had hardly changed—all black and white and shades of gray. His face, however, turned beet red when he looked down at what he was wearing.

"You may be right," he admitted.

Everyone burst into laughter, suddenly filled with relief and joy and exhaustion. Raia's laughter rose above all, loud and clear.

"Raia! We hear you!" exclaimed Olly.

Raia stopped and scowled. "Stop staring!" she snapped. But she couldn't keep her face from breaking into a wide grin.

"I will send a messenger with the four pearls immediately," said Eleyna as they stepped out from the cave. Through the trees, they could see a small crowd of people gathered just outside the great hall. She nodded toward them. "It appears Alexander cast the same spell on the people who live and work here as he did Elias."

"We will return the pearls ourselves," said Horatio.

"But you must be exhausted after your adventures," protested the enchantress. "Stay and rest."

"You are very gracious, Enchantress, but I won't be at peace unless I am sure the lands are well and the pearls are back where they belong."

"Then at least allow my people to prepare some food and supplies for you to take on your journey."

Horatio was about to object, but Eleyna set her hand on his shoulder before he could say anything further. "I won't take no for an answer, Sir Horatio," she said firmly.

Looking at her determined expression, Horatio simply nodded and bowed.

"Good! I'm glad that's settled," said Eleyna. "Olly, please advise Elias on what you will need for your journey. And Sir Horatio, while he does that . . . and maybe has a little snack"—she winked at Olly, whose stomach had been grumbling loudly—"you can spend a few minutes visiting my home. I think there will be many ancient artifacts of interest to you."

"Thank you, Miss Eleyna," replied Horatio.

"Excellent," Eleyna said, smiling. "Elias, why don't you help Olly take the mulions to the stable?"

"Of course." Elias bowed to the adventurers. "Thank you," he said. "So much. You have given me back my life, and my sister. We are indebted to you."

"There's one thing I want to know," said Horatio as Elias and Olly fetched the mulions from the cave. "How did Alexander come to possess the ring?"

Eleyna gazed sadly at the burning ashes that marked where Alexander had stood. "Soon after we married, Alexander asked me about the ring. He wanted to know about my past." She turned to Horatio. "Alexander was my husband. I believed him. So I led him to the mountain and told him most everything—about my family,

the ring, and the pearls. I hoped we could rule together."
She shook her head. "But once he knew he had my trust and
no one was nearby to help, he tricked me into removing the
ring and then trapped me in that dark room. With my
powers so diminished, I couldn't interfere with his plans.
But even while I wore the ring, I didn't really *see* what was
going on, did I? I guess it's easy to fool a fool."

"Stop your nonsense," chided Horatio. "You were
no more foolish than the rest of us were."

"But I endangered the land *I* am supposed to
protect. I should never have left the mountain."

"That's a horrible thing to say," Tommy said
angrily. "You shouldn't be stuck here forever! You didn't
mean to. You just trusted the wrong person."

Eleyna smiled gratefully. "I appreciate that,
Tommy. I really do." She tousled his hair. "I'm honestly not
sure what we would have done without you. I had given up
all hope until you tumbled through that door!" She laughed.
"It seems that Tuddleby trait you told me about is a good
thing, yes?"

Tommy shrugged but felt pleased.

AS ELIAS ORGANIZED PROVISIONS FOR THE RETURN
journey, Olly rejoined them on a quick tour of the great hall,
which was, as they expected, very luxurious. Ancient script
was etched into the rich wood paneling, tapestries hung
over several of the walls, and carved fixtures decorated the

ceilings. As Eleyna had promised, everywhere they found ornaments from centuries past, some of which they suspected had magical qualities.

As they wandered in and out of the various rooms, Tommy gathered up his courage.

"Horatio, Olly," he said resolutely, looking from one to the other. "I have something to tell you."

"Yes m'boy," Horatio chirped. Neither Tommy nor Olly had seen the little man in a better mood.

"About my not being a magician—"

"Oh that!" interrupted Olly. "We didn't believe any of it."

"You didn't?"

"Of course not! It would have been ridiculous of us to doubt you just because of what Alexander said. After all, both Horatio and I *saw* your magic. Alexander was only jealous. If it weren't for you, we would never have found out he was the pearl thief. You saved everyone. Didn't he, Sir Horatio?"

Horatio smiled and nodded.

"I'm still hungry," announced Olly. "Does anyone want anything?"

Horatio rolled his eyes. "Olly, didn't you just have a snack?"

"Well, now that this whole ordeal is behind us, I feel *so* much better! My stomach's back open for business!" Olly replied cheerfully, and he disappeared in the direction of the kitchen.

Tommy laughed. "Good luck, Horatio! I see many sandwiches in your future."

Horatio grinned. "I think you're right."

Tommy took in a slow breath. "Horatio . . ." he said again.

Horatio looked up from a figurine he had been examining, caught by Tommy's serious tone. "Yes?"

"I'm not who you think I am."

"No? You're not Tommy Tuddleby?"

"Yes, I am, but—"

"You are the same Tommy we've been traveling with since we left Rolokon?"

"Yes, but I'm not a magician."

"You mean, you're not Thomas Tuddleby, wayfaring wizard of whimsy, magic maker and spell breaker?"

"I mean both!" said Tommy, frustrated. "I-I'm sorry. I should have said something when I figured it out. At first I thought I was dreaming, and then I knew I wasn't. But then you were so worried. And Olly. And Queen Violet. And . . . and I didn't want to let you down. And you really believed in me—"

"Tommy," Horatio quietly interjected. "Enough. You may not be the person we wanted you to be at first. And perhaps you don't have all the magical abilities a wizard should have. But you are a magic maker, and a wayfaring one at that. Olly's right. Without you, we would never have been able to save the lands. Yes, you should have told us when you realized our mistake. But if we had paid attention, we would have realized it didn't make much sense that the legendary wizard we were looking for was a young boy." He smiled ruefully. "We were so desperate, we didn't want to hear the truth. You were simply trying to live up to our expectations. So we owe you an apology as well. And I *am* sorry."

"Are you going to tell Olly? I'm worried he'll be disappointed in me."

"I don't think so," said Olly, reappearing at the doorway. Tommy and Horatio swung around.

"You heard?" Tommy asked.

"I heard enough," said Olly. He set his plate of food down on a side table, walked over to Tommy, and swallowed him up in a warm embrace. "I could never be disappointed in you, my friend."

Horatio cleared his throat. Tommy looked up and saw Raia standing by the doorway. Olly stood up straight and turned around. "Raia! Oh dear!"

"It's all right, Olly," said Tommy sheepishly. "She knows."

They looked from Tommy to Raia in surprise. "But how . . ."

"I figured it out back at the cave when the tree fell on Tommy," Raia replied. She handed him his satchel and added, "Here, I figured you'd want this."

"How *did* you get out, Tommy?" asked Horatio.

Tommy removed his pocketknife from the satchel and held it up to them. "Raia saw the knife cuts in the branches and knew that's how I'd escaped."

"He made me promise not to tell anyone . . . and under the circumstances, that wasn't a hard promise to keep!" Raia said, grinning. The other three laughed.

At that moment, Eleyna entered the room. Tommy glanced over at her and then back to Horatio. "Horatio, is there any way I could go home sooner than we planned?"

"But why?" Olly asked. "Don't you want to see Queen Violet? She'll be expecting you!"

"I think what Tommy means is that he'd love to stay," Eleyna assured Olly, "but now that the pearls are found, he must return home."

Tommy nodded.

"Do you have your top hat?" asked Horatio.

Tommy's face sank. "I didn't think . . . it's in the palace—"

"Why don't you stay with me tonight," suggested Eleyna. "I'm sure we have much to talk about, and I'll make sure you return home by the morning."

Too soon, Horatio, Raia, and Olly bid Tommy a tearful goodbye.

"Will we never see you again?" wept the color guard.

"I don't know, Olly," Tommy replied. He hugged his friend tightly. "But I'll never forget either you or Horatio."

Tommy embraced Raia next. "I couldn't have done any of this without you, Raia. You've been a really good friend, and I'm going to miss you a lot."

Raia returned the big hug. This time it didn't seem so weird. "Me too." She stepped back. "And next time you won't get to do all the talking."

"Next time . . . I hope so," Tommy said wistfully.

Eleyna took Raia's hands in her own, saying, "You were remarkable, Raia. Truly." Raia blushed and lowered her head. "Perhaps you would like to visit me sometime?" Raia looked up, startled. "Elias and I could certainly use the company!"

Raia beamed. "Really? That . . . that would be wonderful. Thank you!"

"Good!" Eleyna smiled. "We will make arrangements so the journey isn't so long . . . or eventful . . . next time!"

The three travelers mounted their mulions. Eleyna had suggested that Kia remain at Rhian for when Tommy returned. Everyone agreed that was an excellent idea. "You have done a great service for the kingdom of Aesteron, Tommy Tuddleby," said Horatio, sitting tall on his mulion. "In the name of the queen, I proclaim you an honorary member of the royal council." He removed his top hat and bowed.

And with those last words, Horatio, Olly, and Raia disappeared down the mountain road.

The Wayfaring Wizard of Whimsy

I imagine you would still like to know about your wristband," said Eleyna as they walked back to the great hall. "I thought it best to tell you when we were alone."

Tommy stopped and took a deep breath. "He's your dad, isn't he?" said Tommy.

The enchantress looked at him, surprised. "Who?"

"My Uncle Thomas."

Eleyna paused and slowly nodded. They resumed walking. "However did you know?"

"Well, he had a book in his house. It was the same one Olly told us about. The *Book of El . . .*"

"Eldred. Yes. It tells the history of our family going back more than two centuries."

"Right. And Olly told us a story about this stranger who fell in love with the daughter of an enchanter, and how the stranger would visit the land from a faraway place. And then . . . well . . . your hair. Uncle Thomas's hair is light brown, but Aunt Red, she's got hair just like yours!"

"Aunt Red?"

"Sorry. I mean Rej."

"You mean Rejeena?" Eleyna's eyes lit up. "You've met my mother? Of course you have! Is she well?"

"So that's her name! She's good. They travel a lot. They moved to Colorado."

"Colorado?"

"Yeah. It's a place with a lot of mountains. But now that I think of it, Aunt Red often does look kind of sad. Don't they come here to see you? And Elias?"

"Oh yes. But it's been a couple of years. You see, time works differently between our two worlds. A month here is but a weekend in your world."

"So that's where they go! Every month, they go away for a weekend. One time I asked if I could come too, and Uncle Thomas said it was a secret vacation spot where just he and Aunt Red get to go. That must have been here!"

"Yes. They normally come once each year, but last year and the year before they did not. Something about moving. I guess to that place—Colorado." Eleyna shook her head sadly. "Maybe if they had come, this wouldn't have happened. My grandfather was here when they left, but then he thought it time for him to . . . to retire. Everyone thought I could handle things, that I'd look out for my little brother and Rhian and the kingdom . . ." Eleyna shook her head sadly. "But clearly they expected too much. I guess Alexander could see that even without the ring."

Tommy rolled his eyes. "What did I tell you before? Stop blaming yourself for everything! That's a lot to handle! Hey, I just thought of something really weird. Because time works differently, does that mean you're actually older than your dad at this point?"

"I'd never thought of that, but I guess . . . yes, yes, I am. The time he spent here aged him—that's why he started spending less time at Rhian. It's all a bit . . . complicated."

"One thing I really don't get, though. Why did he give *me* the band if it was so important?" asked Tommy.

"My grandfather gave it to my father when he came back the second time—after he helped battle the sorcerer—in case we ever needed him aga—"

"He battled the sorcerer?" Tommy interrupted excitedly. "It was all real?"

"You know about the sorcerer?"

"Yeah! In the story Olly told us, a sorcerer kidnapped the enchanter's daughter . . . but I thought *that* was just to, you know, spice things up." Tommy grinned.

"Well, there are a few stories, but yes, the sorcerer was real."

"That is just so cool!" Tommy bounced, his eyes wide. "I mean, what happened? That was your mom, wasn't it? And your dad, he was the messenger, right? The one who distributed all the pearls the first time?"

"Yes and yes, when he was about your age . . . wait, do you want to hear about your wristband or not?"

"Sorry . . ."

Eleyna laughed. "The wristband only opens the portal in your bedroom. It sends out a signal that allowed Horatio to find you. After my father saved my mother—"

"From that sorcerer?" Tommy said.

"Yes," Eleyna said, amused. "When that happened, my grandfather gave my father—your uncle—a different device that allowed him to come and go between my world and yours from anywhere. I sometimes think Granddad was hoping my father and mother would fall in love and was just trying to make it easy for them to see each other. I guess it worked, because that's exactly what happened!"

"That's what Olly said! But why didn't Horatio just call Uncle . . . your dad this time?"

"I'm honestly not sure how Horatio even knew to reach you through the portal! Now that Granddad is gone, only I know how to reach my father and mother."

"Horatio said it was written in some instructions from a really long time ago. That in case of emergency, they should contact Thomas Tuddleby, wayfaring wizard of whimsy, magic maker and spellbreaker!"

Eleyna chuckled. "That sounds like something my father would have said. He probably left the instructions to the ruler of Aesteron after the first pearl theft in Rolokon."

"The *first* theft?"

"Ah, nice to see there's something you *don't* know."

"Can Uncle Thomas even do magic?"

"Not that I know of . . . though maybe my mother has been able to teach him a thing or two."

"So everyone here forgot about this," Tommy said, pointing to the wristband, "including you. Which is why you never told Alexander about it and he had no idea that there was another way to get help from outside the land."

"Exactly." Eleyna nodded.

"And my uncle assumed no one would ever have reason to use his old band, so it was safe with me. Oh boy! I bet he'll be surprised when he finds out what happened!"

Eleyna chuckled. "You can say that again!"

"Gosh. No one would believe this! Can I tell Uncle Thomas I know his secret? I don't have to tell them *every*thing. Some things should be just between cousins, right?" he quickly added.

Eleyna smiled. "Of course, Tommy. Though they might have quite a bit to say to me when they next visit! Part of growing up, though, right?" She wrapped her arm around his shoulders as they walked. "I think I hear your stomach growling. How about we have some dinner?"

Tommy nodded.

"Tell me everything you like."

TANTALIZING AROMAS FILLED THE AIR AS TOMMY, ELIAS, and Eleyna sat down at a large table piled high with platters of meat, stuffing, fresh-baked breads, sugared berries, and pies of every kind. The staff of the great hall and their families had been invited to join in and celebrate their restored freedom. It was all delicious, but Tommy could hardly stay awake.

After the meal, Eleyna led him up to a room where he could rest. He snuggled up under layers of warm blankets, and the enchantress sat on the edge of the bed.

"Eleyna, how are you going to send me home?"

"Go to sleep. When you wake up, you'll be back in your own bed."

"Mom and Dad are probably so mad at me. I've been away for over a week!"

Eleyna shook her head. "I don't think so, Tommy. Remember, time works differently here. In your world, you've only been away for one night. Everything will be fine."

"Eleyna, what are *you* going to do?"

"What will I do?" She paused, musing. "I'm going to think about all that's happened, I guess. There's a lot to think about!"

"Then what? Will you ever leave the mountain again?"

"Life wouldn't be very interesting if I didn't, would it? Though I'm hoping next time won't be quite as interesting as these past few weeks!"

"Oh, before I forget—" Tommy removed the magical wristband. "Here." He placed it in the palm of her hand. "You might need it someday."

Eleyna looked down at it, rubbing her thumb along its smooth surface. Then she kissed his forehead, blew out the candle that lit the room, and left.

Within moments, Tommy fell fast asleep.

Home Again

There was a light tapping on the door. Tommy's eyes fluttered open. The door squeaked ajar.

"Tommy, are you awake yet? It's nearly ten a.m.!" The door opened wider. "Have you been sleeping all this time?" His mother stood at the doorway, holding a stack of folded towels.

It had worked! He was home, and Rhian was like a faraway dream.

"I was pretty tired, Mom."

She glanced around the room. "Obviously not from cleaning." She bent down and scooped up a wrinkled shirt, then walked over and kissed his forehead. She stood back. "Tommy, are you still in your clothes from yesterday?!"

Surprised, Tommy extended his arms and peeked under the covers to see his legs. He was indeed wearing the same clothes as the day he'd left. He was glad to have them back, but kind of sad too. He sighed. "Like I said, I was really tired."

"Oh," his mother responded, a speck of doubt in her voice. "And don't you think it's time you get a watch that tells proper time? At least one that has numbers you can read."

Tommy sat up, startled. "Mom?"

But she was already on her way out of the room. "Breakfast will be ready soon," she called back to him.

He looked down and saw the band strapped around his wrist. As he pushed back the blanket, he hit something at the foot of the bed. His satchel. He'd left it on his chair at dinner. Thank goodness Eleyna had remembered! Unless . . . maybe she hadn't.

He took in a deep breath. His clothes. The wristband. Like he'd never left. *What if it was all a dream and none of it was real? There must be* some*thing!*

Tommy turned the satchel upside down on the bed. Everything tumbled out: the high-resolution compact binoculars, the seven-in-one survival whistle, the five-in-one pocketknife, the Spy Right invisible pen with UV blacklight key chain and a pad of paper. No Pop Rocks, but that could've been part of the dream too. Maybe he only *thought* he'd put them in his bag. It didn't prove anything. He shook the satchel again. Nothing. His face fell.

He climbed out of bed and went to his desk, unstrapped the wristband, opened the top drawer, and tossed it in. Then he went to put everything back in his satchel. When he opened it, though, something caught his eye. Tommy opened the bag wider and saw a crumpled piece of paper caught in a zipped pocket. He smoothed the paper as best he could. It was blank.

Trembling, he pointed the blacklight at it.

I'll miss you, wayfaring wizard.
Come back soon.
Your friend, Raia

He unzipped the pocket and found six empty Pop Rocks packages. Tommy grinned. He retrieved the band and refastened it around his wrist.

'Cause like Jake Jones always says, "Adventure awaits those who dare. Just make darned sure you come prepared!"

The End